"You'll be my

The only way to be a father to his son was to persuade Robyn to marry him. And that meant Robyn would be his wife. In every way. Corey wasn't a man to accept half measures and he certainly wouldn't settle for a marriage in-name-only to a woman who still made him burn with desire.

Corey had never proposed to a woman, but he had always assumed that if he asked a woman to marry him, she would happily say yes.

Except Robyn was different. She had that darn stubborn O'Halloran blood running through her.

So Corey would have to find a way to make her love him again. To make her marry him. And all bets were off, both sleeves rolled up, the credit card cocked. He'd charm her and woo her.

And if that didn't work he'd move on to plan B: he'd make love to her.

Dear Reader,

Don your white dress for three special occasions—a christening, a debutante ball and a wedding! In GOWNS OF WHITE, three favorite American Romance authors prove that "No one can resist a woman in white!"

Vivian Leiber revisits the night Robyn O'Halloran became a deb—and a woman, at the hands of Corey Harte. In the dark of night there were no secrets between them, but now, years later, Corey's about to discover one.

Vivian grew up when being a debutante wasn't cool, when brides were as likely to wear love beads as pearls, and when nobody knew what the christening gown in grandma's attic was for. But while she didn't go to any cotillions and her bridal gown has long since faded to antique yellow, she has always been proud to be an old-fashioned gal. Vivian lives in a small Illinois town where she enjoys iced tea on the porch on summer evenings, riding bikes to the ice cream shop with her boys, her husband's first after-work kiss when she picks him up at the train station and curling up with a romance novel on a rainy afternoon.

Next month, be sure to catch the last GOWNS OF WHITE—it's a special presentation by Anne Stuart with *The Right Man.*

Debra Matteucci
Senior Editor & Editorial Coordinator
Harlequin Books
300 East 42nd Street
New York, NY 10017

Secret Daddy

VIVIAN LEIBER

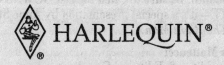

HARLEQUIN®

TORONTO • NEW YORK • LONDON
AMSTERDAM • PARIS • SYDNEY • HAMBURG
STOCKHOLM • ATHENS • TOKYO • MILAN • MADRID
PRAGUE • WARSAW • BUDAPEST • AUCKLAND

ISBN 0-373-16761-X

SECRET DADDY

Chapter One

Dr. Corey Harte stepped off the red-and-gold carpet leading from the curb to the entrance of the Drake Hotel. Around him, in the last moments before the sun went down, swirled a tide of gossamer-gowned women, tourists toting overstuffed bags and cameras, and out-of-town shoppers returning from the Magnificent Mile. The uniformed doormen, bellboys and captains darted this way and that with efficient fanfare—whistling down cabs, helping passengers out of their limousines, hoisting luggage onto the brass carts.

Standing on the curb, Corey scanned the traffic backed up a block in either direction—every vehicle belching exhaust, angry drivers with their heads out of their windows honking and maneuvering inch by inch to a better position for picking up and depositing occupants at the door of the five-star hotel.

''Gotcha,'' a whiskey-rough voice said just as

the flash popped. A gnomelike face with a five-o'clock shadow and fleshy jowls peered over a camera.

"Rusty, give it up," Corey said, glancing down. "When it's newsprint, all men in tuxes look alike."

"Yeah, but with your name under the picture, I get a coupla extra bills in my Friday envelope."

"Why aren't you taking a shot of her?" Corey tilted his head to indicate a young lady emerging from a black stretch limousine with the help of a driver, two bellboys and the captain. The voluminous lace of the woman's snowy white gown caught on the door handle, and for an instant it looked as if she would be hitched forever to the rented limo. A quick-thinking doorman unsnarled the lace and the young lady yanked her dress and her escort into the hotel.

"We did the debutantes' gowns already," Rusty said. "Lined 'em up in the ballroom and got their class picture in the Thursday edition. Looked like brides, they did."

"Don't you think a few extra photos of the ladies would be more newsworthy than another of me?" Corey asked absently, surveying the cars, wondering when she would appear and, when she did, if he would recognize her.

But of course he'd recognize her.

If he could just get the image of her in cutoffs and a T-shirt out of his head. Tonight she'd be wearing a white gown, elbow-length gloves and an upswept hairdo—the uniform of debutantes everywhere.

Even though this particular deb was a housekeeper's daughter.

"Who reads the society page?" Rusty demanded. He fished a flash attachment out of the pocket of his white-and-brown houndstooth jacket. The sun was just setting over Bloomingdale's, and the street was cast in shadow. "Our readers—women or men?"

"Women, I suppose."

"So who do they want to see Monday morning over corn flakes and coffee? A picture of another girl in a white dress or C.M.E.B. filling out a tuxedo just right?"

Corey glanced at Rusty.

"Is that what you call me down at the newsroom?"

"Yeah. Fewer syllables than Chicago's most eligible—"

"I get the idea. What are you going to do when I'm gone? I start my residency in New York tomorrow."

"I'll pine away for you. So will half the population of Chicago—the female half."

"Rusty…"

"Come on, you've always been a decent guy. Let me get a shot of you that'll last my female readers four years. Try to look like that guy—the

Kennedy kid. Could you tousle your hair? Look up—it makes the blue in your eyes come out. Try to look like you're thinking of running for office.''

''No,'' Corey said, unconsciously raking his fingers through hair. ''Rusty, you got your one shot. Now go away.''

Rusty threw back his shoulders and nearly filled out the pads of his jacket. ''I got a right to make my living on this sidewalk. Public property, first amendment and freedom of the press. You're the one who don't belong here. Aren't you assigned by the debutante committee to escort Miss Lelaine Paik, daughter of the Asian banker Sunayim Paik?''

''Yeah, but she's in the powder room adjusting her dress.''

''That'll take forever. My missus can stay in a powder room for an hour and come out looking exactly like what she did when she went in.''

The two men nodded in a solidarity that transcended all their differences.

''I'm just out here…''

''What?''

''Just looking,'' Corey muttered, shaking his head.

''You tell me what you're looking for, I could help you find it. Is it a woman?''

Corey glanced up the street to a white limousine at the corner. A woman in a white debutante dress had apparently tired of waiting for traffic to clear and had climbed out of her limo on her own. As she stepped through the snarling vehicles, holding her hem above the sidewalk, her escort trailed behind, carrying her evening bag and gloves.

''A girl,'' Corey responded to Rusty, realizing it was very hard to think of Robyn as a woman. And yet, of course, she would be by now.

The purpose of a debutante ball was to introduce a girl into society as a woman.

But to Corey, Robyn was skinned knees and pigtails. Robyn was the crack of her bat against a baseball in summer and making snowmen in the barren garden in winter. Robyn was a kid, a girl, a youngster forever in blue jeans—wasn't she?

''Friend of the family,'' Corey said, shoving his hands deep, way deep, in his pockets. ''Haven't seen her in four years. Went away to boarding school. But she's coming back tonight.''

''Would that be the O'Halleran girl?''

''Yes.'' Corey's eyes narrowed. ''Just what do you know about her?''

''The usual gossip—she's the daughter of your father's former housekeeper. Some say there was a little hanky-panky there.''

''My father loved her mother,'' Corey admitted. ''They might have married, but she died.''

''And he's spent an awful lot of moolah putting her daughter through a fancy boarding school out East, paying for clothes, for braces...''

''Robyn's never needed braces.''

"Still, the idea is he gave the little girl the Cinderella treatment. Laid down a hundred grand to make the debutante committee send her an invite. And tonight Cinderella's coming home," Rusty eyed him speculatively. "Are you thinking of being her prince?"

"No way," Corey said. "And stop loading that film."

"I gotta—"

"Don't. She's a girl—just a little girl."

"A little girl?" Rusty whistled. "I didn't know they let little girls into the deb ball."

"Okay, so she's eighteen."

"State of Illinois calls that a woman. Age of consent and all."

Corey glared at him. "Last I saw of her, she was fourteen, and she didn't even like boys."

"Not even you?"

"Not even me," Corey answered with not quite so much assurance. "I was seven years older than her, more like a brother."

"Take it from me, buddy," Rusty said. He tugged his camera strap over an uncomfortable spot on his shoulder. "I got three kids. A lot can happen to a girl in four years."

"Rusty, nice talking to you, but I gotta—"

"No, don't walk away," Rusty said, breaking into a gallop to catch up with Corey's stride. "I'm stickin' to you like glue. A girl immune to

C.M.E.B.'s charms. Whoo-ee! I'm definitely getting a bonus in my Friday envelope.''

"I'M SCARED," Robyn confessed, smoothing her dress over her lap. For the zillionth time since traffic had sputtered to a stop a half block from the hotel, she slid the smoky window of the limousine down and craned her neck out to see.

"You should be scared," Ashford Pinksmith III said mildly. He smoothed his glistening hair back from his face with a sterling comb. "At the debutante ball, they release caged African tigers who haven't been fed in weeks. Specially trained ones who have been raised on chickens wrapped in white tulle."

Robyn pulled her head back into the limousine and narrowed her green eyes at the man seated on the jumpseat across from her. Ashford had been assigned by the cotillion ball committee to be her escort, and Robyn, having never met the freckle-faced heir to a lightbulb factory, wasn't sure what to make of him.

"You're joking," she said.

"Of course I'm joking," he said. "Robyn, this is my tenth or eleventh debutante ball, and every gal gets nervous, every gal gets excited and scared, every gal freaks when it's time to curtsy."

"I'm not nervous about the curtsy. I've been practicing."

The cotillion ball required a floor-touching

curtsy as each debutante was presented to the guests in a ceremony that had sent generations of debs into fits of panic.

"If you've been practicing the curtsy," Ashford inquired, "what's there to be nervous about?"

"I don't know," she said. "Come on, I'm getting claustrophobic. We can walk."

"In those heels?" Ashford asked doubtfully, eyeing her *peau de soie* slippers. "They're as delicate as rose petals and there are oil slicks and potholes and—hey! Robyn, wait for me!"

Out on the street, Robyn tugged her dress, wiggling just a little at the hips to allow the hem to fall around her ankles. Aunt Rose's creation didn't boast a bustle or a train or a flounce or even a seemingly de rigeur trail of tulle. Aunt Rose didn't have the money for that kind of dress and Robyn was loath to ask Dr. Harte for even a penny more of his generosity.

Aunt Rose had created a dress with nine yards of handkerchief linen, hand-pleated and nipped in at the waist with a single swath of paper-light Garrickmacross lace. Robyn had flown in from school Tuesday, just missing the "class photo" opportunity at the Drake Ballroom. But looking at the other debs' gowns over her aunt's shoulder at the society page of the Tribune on Thursday morning had confirmed what she had always suspected— Aunt Rose was a magician with a bolt of fabric and a little bit of lace.

Why did she still repair suits and take up hems for a living when she had this gift?

The crowd gathering at the Drake for the debutante ball was a tough one to impress, but Robyn enjoyed the head swivels as she waded through stalled cabs and grumbling limos.

And why shouldn't she enjoy the attention?

Stuck for four years at a boarding school out East—a girls' school where Friday nights were for chemistry lab and long weekends for catching up on math homework. Most of her classmates plotted a future that included medical school, law school, joining the diplomatic corps or heading up a multinational corporation.

Robyn figured the career ambition gene was simply not part of her DNA even as she did her best to keep up with her studies. Because when she envisioned her future, all she saw was a home and children. Lots of children.

Oh, of course, she'd have to have a husband. And that was what a cotillion ball was for—to present young women to society as officially available with a capital *A*. It was an old-fashioned custom, but Dr. Harte had told her that he wanted her to go, because her mother had asked him before her death to give Robyn the chance.

The older doctor had written to her with the news that the cotillion ball committee had invited her and included his strong recommendation that she find herself a husband from the evening's eligible men. Robyn thought it sounded a little cold-blooded to plot and plan, but she fully intended to enjoy herself.

Tough to enjoy things when you're scared and nervous and don't even know why.

But she had practiced her curtsy and read three etiquette books so that she would make Dr. Harte proud. She knew which fork to use, when to take off her white elbow-length gloves, how to waltz and how to introduce herself to others.

Still...

This afternoon she had been so jumpy that Aunt Rose despaired while trying to put mascara on her lashes. So tightly wound that Robyn couldn't keep her hairpins in place and already had a tendril of coppery curls cascading down her exposed shoulders. The limo ride had been torture in her over-anxious state. And now as she threaded her way through the traffic jam, she could barely keep from breaking into a full-throttle run toward the hotel.

A pothole, reasonably sized for Chicago, but larger than tolerated in most municipalities, caught the heel of her shoe.

Her ankle twisted—pain as sharp and sure as lightning raced up her leg—but she righted herself before injury.

And then turned to look at the disaster.

At the bottom of the pothole, lay the small, finely crafted shoe, a smear of oil across its toe.

She hiked up her dress even farther, exposing a

slim, pale leg hosed in shimmering silk. She hesitated. If she put her foot down on the asphalt, the stocking would be ruined.

She looked at her official escort, who was three cars back giving instructions to their driver.

Darn it! Double darn it! Her worst weakness—jumping into things headlong and then having the leisure to enjoy the ensuing catastrophe.

"Here, let me help," a smooth, somehow familiar voice said at her shoulder. Then the dark-haired, formally dressed man knelt at her feet, and Robyn put her hand on his shoulder to steady herself.

He rescued her shoe and cupped it against her pale, silk-stockinged foot.

Then and only then, did he look up.

Robyn stared openmouthed.

Corey returned her stare.

How could he have become a man while she felt she had remained merely a child?

A flash popped in her face, and she put her arm over her eyes to shield them from a second one.

"Rusty, stop it!" Corey ordered.

Robyn put her arm down as the diminutive photographer groused that America wouldn't last until the next millennium if there wasn't freedom of the press. Nonetheless, he directed his attention toward another limousine disgorging its passengers.

Robyn barely noticed him leave, so entranced was she by Corey. It was Corey. Her Corey. He held her slim ankle in his left hand while with a linen handkerchief he wiped the worst of the damage off her shoe. Peering over her uplifted skirt, Robyn reached out to touch his face, to caress his hair—perhaps only to confirm that he was Corey, or maybe to fulfill a sudden directive from deep within her.

She started to lose her balance, although perhaps it was just the excitement of the night or the dizzying turn of the earth in its orbit.

Ashford Pinksmith III caught up to her, steadying her by the elbow.

Corey stood, a good six inches taller than her, even with her heels on. His shoulder muscles strained at the ebony jacket that otherwise hung with tailored precision.

And, leaning forward ever so slightly she smelled woodruff and musk, the scent of manhood so baffling and yet alluring to her cloistered senses.

"Wow," Corey said, looking her up and down and up again.

"At last, a Harte man rendered completely inarticulate," Ashford said. "This is like a down-home family reunion for you two."

"Robyn, you've…grown up," Corey said. "You're not a little girl anymore."

Robyn opened her mouth, a smart reply just aching to be spoken. She had never let Corey get away with acting as if he were older, faster, smarter or better at batting a ball.

Even if he was.

But her mind, so quick four years ago at making comebacks, simply shut down. She felt an unaccountable urge to throw back her shoulders and display herself, as if she were a treasure to be won by only the best of men.

To be won by him.

"Hi, Corey," she said, holding his stare for an instant and then, as if that photographer were around to blind her with his flash camera, dropping her gaze to the ground.

Great, she thought, *you're sounding like a breathless Marilyn Monroe impersonator. Can't you say something a little more intelligent?*

"The two of you are utterly scintillating in conversation," Ashford said dryly, drawing Robyn toward the curb. "But while you're considering discussing astrophysics or world peace or whatever other deep topic interests you, I'll remind you that you're blocking traffic. Come along, Robyn. Oh, don't worry, you'll see Corey again soon."

"I will?" she asked, suddenly realizing that seeing Corey, seeing a lot of Corey, was presently the most important goal in the world.

"Yes, because I owe him," Ashford said. "Two years ago a certain young lady was making her debut, and Corey here was assigned to escort her. I was so consumed with adoration that I persuaded Corey to let me switch place cards so I could sit next to her at dinner."

"Then what happened?" Robyn asked. Though she kept her gaze firmly on Corey who walked at her other side, she had never been able to resist a good story. "What happened next?"

"There was no next," Ashford said. "We had a delightful affair that lasted for several weeks and then her parents sent her to Europe. Because while I am a nice cad, I am nonetheless a cad."

"A cad?"

"Absolutely. And parents are rightfully wary of me. I would have used my considerable charm to take advantage of her. But alas, after she got on that plane, I never heard from her again. Corey, you have my permission to switch the place cards, but Robyn, you have to at least walk in with me. Won't look right otherwise. Put your gloves on, young lady."

Robyn felt an absence at her side. She turned her head as Ashford guided her up the gold-and-ruby-carpeted steps of the hotel.

Corey lingered at the curb, watching her.

Their eyes met, and she hoped she saw in them a promise that he would find her again.

She felt oddly bereft, and now her head throbbed with worry—what if Corey didn't switch place cards? What if he didn't seek her out again? Did he feel anything for her, something beyond a vaguely remembered brotherly affection?

She took one glove from Ashford and pulled it on, buttoning the twelve seed pearls at the wrist.

Now she knew what had kept her tense and jumpy as she had prepared for the ball. She had known she would be meeting destiny, and that destiny would be Corey Harte.

AT THE CURB, Corey Harte stood in silent contemplation until the very last glimpse of coppery hair and ivory skin disappeared within the Drake's lobby.

Robyn O'Halleran had grown up.

Four years had taken a skinned kneed, gawky-faced, wild-maned tomboy and made her into a woman. The kind of woman that asserted her feminine powers without saying a word—with just a look, an innocent enough glance, that made a man's groin ache and his fingers tremble with the need to touch, to hold, to caress, to possess.

He had touched her ankle, held her foot in the palm of his hand, had overcome the urge to glide his fingers along the silky leg. And yet touching Robyn should be no different than, for instance, years earlier hoisting her on his shoulders so she could see over the crowd at the Fourth of July parade.

But now, touching her, smelling her scent of ivory soap and vanilla had all the innocence of a late-night cable television movie.

Corey had had his successes with women, even women of great feminine charm and cachet. A few brief affairs—hell, he'd be the first to admit they were often little more than one-night stands. But always he entered into these liaisons without any promises or lies. And when the women exited his life, they took with them a feeling of having been thoroughly and completely made love to and with a certain wistful regret that timing hadn't allowed for anything long-term.

Even as Corey felt the masculine desire to seduce Robyn, he also felt a familiar protectiveness. When she had lived with her mother in the carriage house behind the Harte mansion, Corey had been Robyn's most ardent protector. Had talked sternly to the third-grade bully who hassled her on her way home from school—seven years age difference meant he didn't have to use his fists. Had warned away many punks who had wanted to make Robyn, as she entered her teens, their steady—somehow Corey had found something unsuitable about every one of them.

If Corey was being the Corey of ten minutes ago, he'd warn himself away from Robyn right now. He'd walk right down Michigan Avenue and cool off on the North Avenue Pier. He'd tell himself that whatever he had in mind—and he had a lot in mind—was out of the question. And he'd back up his words with a fist if he had to.

After all, he wasn't suitable. He had never been the kind of man to take his time with long, puppy-faced, lovey-dovey looks and hours of chaste hand-holding. He would overwhelm her. But much more important, he didn't have a future to offer, especially with his four-year residency at the toughest hospital program in New York beginning the next day. And she deserved more—much more—she deserved her fresh-faced enthusiasm and innocence, all the experiences of carefree youth.

Go, he warned himself. *Get the hell out of here. Beat it!*

But instead Corey walked past white-gowned women and their escorts milling in the corridor into the atrium ballroom, past a gaggle of waiters arguing over the placement of the wineglasses. He located the table assigned to Ashford and Robyn and the one where he and Lelaine were to be seated.

He switched the place cards and knew he could trust Ashford to tell Lelaine that he, not Corey, had asked for the switch. He smiled wryly as he thought of Ashford dropping his head guiltily as if expecting Lelaine to scold him—and then rousing himself for a mischievous wink that would make Lelaine laugh.

And then Corey thought of himself seated next to Robyn.

Don't. he warned himself.

He reached to the card with his name on it to switch it back, and then rationalized—*at least if she's seated next to me, I can protect her from other men*—and before he could change his mind or puncture holes in his own logic, he strode out of the ballroom.

Chapter Two

"Okay, buddy, this makes us even," Ashford said as he held Robyn's chair for her.

Lelaine Paik, slender and winsome in a simple white satin gown, narrowed her eyes at Corey.

"What does he mean by that?"

Ashford took Lelaine's arm.

"Lelaine, darling," he said contritely, leading her away from the table, "I've done something very, very naughty."

"Really? Ashford, I'd hardly think you the type to do anything out of line," Lelaine said, winking at Corey and Robyn.

"Oh, but I am. And Corey was kind enough not to scold me. I hope you won't be too stern with me when I confess...I switched the place cards."

Robyn and Corey found themselves on opposite sides of the gilt dining chair. Around them, debs were finding their seats, parents proudly took candid shots with disposable cameras they slipped out of evening bags, harried escorts were sent to retrieve misplaced gloves and drinks. One hundred waiters, two for each table, were pouring wine and urging guests to sit down. Still, Robyn and Corey couldn't have been more isolated than if the grand dining room of the Drake had only one table and two chairs.

"Somehow I never expected you to grow up," Corey said in wonder. "I walked out on that curb tonight and kept looking for a little girl in blue jean cutoffs and a ponytail."

"I'm a woman now," Robyn insisted, and then softened, knowing tonight wasn't the time for the good-natured—sometimes not so good-natured—ribbing and joking and arguing that they had grown up with. She had a new and sudden awareness of her femininity, one that was best suited to a softly confident voice. Yet his approval was important. "Did I turn out all right?"

"More than all right," he assured her.

He helped her into her seat, asked her about school and opened her napkin onto her lap before remembering that he hadn't done that since she was seven and she was an adult now, perfectly capable of doing it herself.

While he appropriately turned to the woman seated at his other side to make small talk, he would never again in his life remember what he said, what she said or even what she looked like. Instead, the greater part of him was with Robyn—

and when it came time for the first dance, he took Robyn's hand with relief.

He felt her tiny waist in his hands and realized then that the expected three inches of space between deb and escort was miles too wide. He was crazy drunk with wanting—and he hadn't had a sip of anything stronger than soda. How could she be so calm, so bewitchingly calm?

Perhaps she wasn't—for as she lifted her face to smile at him, her cheeks were flushed the subtle pink of tea roses.

"When I was fourteen, I had a crush on you," she said. "Even if you were an overbearing, know-it-all, arrogant son of a—"

"I was never any of that," he said with a smile that showed her he knew he'd been exactly that. Four years ago, he'd just gotten out of college and was about to start medical school, and he *knew* there wasn't anything he couldn't do. Med school had punched some of that out of him—between the long hours, tough studies and the glimpse of the life-and-death struggles of everyday medicine. Or maybe moving into his mid-twenties had shown him his own limitation and had engendered in him a healthy respect for other people.

"Do you still have the crush?"

"I had hoped four years at boarding school would have cured me," she said, and then added dreamily, "Corey, do you believe in destiny?"

''I do now,'' he said, and in that instant he could have cursed his own voice.

He was leaving for New York tomorrow, for four years of a grueling one-hundred-hour-a-week hospital schedule that would seldom include time for sleep, much less a fresh relationship.

He wouldn't, he mustn't, he couldn't make promises.

And yet he couldn't help but shove tomorrow aside when now he had Robyn in his arms.

''We don't have to stay,'' she said. Her meaning was unmistakable.

No, he thought, *I've got to say no for both of us.*

And yet, saying no was the most difficult task he had ever undertaken. But say no he did, and set himself up for a challenging evening. To dance with her but close his ears to the romance of the music. To drink champagne with her, but not kiss the lips that touched the shared glass. To put his arm around her waist, but hold his hand poised between contraction and release. To applaud her curtsy before the assembled guests—and to know that it was his buddy Ashford who had the honor of presenting her. To take his turn presenting Lelaine under the blazing spotlight, even as his eyes searched for Robyn in the line of white dresses and tuxedos.

As the evening wore on, his self-discipline ran

ragged. When she put her hand inside his jacket to rest her hand on his chest, he groaned aloud.

When her head found the hollow between is shoulder bone and deltoid muscle, he felt a certain tether break.

And when she stood up on tiptoe to whisper in his ear that she wanted to go now, well...

Quite simply, he lost it.

"Robyn, you want what?"

Her mouth was so close to his earlobe that her breath sent shivers up and down his spine.

"I want to go. With you. Please."

He knew it cost her to ask. It wasn't easy for any woman to be so bold. Particularly a woman as young and untried as Robyn.

"I have a room upstairs," he admitted, hearing his more controlled self saying "No!" as if from a very far distance. "The balls often run into the next morning, and I didn't want to have to drive home."

"Take me there," she said. "Please."

He guided her from the ballroom, catching Ashford's eye as he danced with Lelaine. Ashford pantomimed from behind her back a single question: "Do I drive Lelaine home, buddy?"

Corey nodded.

Ashford made an okay sign and waved goodbye.

Corey caught up with Robyn just outside the ballroom in the wide hallway, lined with French provincial chairs and occasional tables.

The lighting was harsh compared to the soft glow of the ballroom, the scent of flowers and expensive perfume was not nearly so intoxicating, and the brisk salute of the bellboy standing at the elevator should have brought Corey to his senses.

In fact, as he entered the empty elevator with Robyn, he was about to tell her that it would be a mistake to make love this evening, however magical the evening might be, that while they certainly had something going on between them that was more intense than a schoolgirl crush—hell, he knew this woman almost as well as he knew himself, and for the first time in his life, Corey was thinking about the *M*-word—there were four years of a residency for Corey to complete, a residency that wouldn't allow for a relationship. And he wouldn't want her to think she was supposed to put her life on hold while waiting for him to pull his together.

He was just about to tell her that she was the most damnably beautiful woman he had ever seen, and that perhaps their destiny was truly being forged this night, but that he shouldn't, she shouldn't, they shouldn't, when—

"If you don't kiss me, I'll have to kiss you," Robyn said. And she threw her arms around him, coming at him with all the grace and savoir faire of an enthusiastic puppy.

"Whoa, Robyn," he said, using one hand to

hold her steady and the other to hang onto the railing. "Kissing isn't a wrestling contest."

Robyn bristled at the suggestion, however true, that she didn't have a lot of experience.

"Let me show you, baby," he said. "Like this. Close your eyes."

When his lips touched hers, lightly first and then deeper, she felt herself slipping as if the marble floor of the elevator were rain-slickened. She gripped his arms and let her head fall back so that she could take his tongue between her lips. He touched and teased her flesh, and she responded, reveling in the new sensations, like fireworks at her nerve endings of her mouth.

How her whole body ached for his touch!

When the bell rang and the doors of the elevator opened, he relinquished her and she wavered.

"Robyn, did you have anything to drink?" he asked.

"Just the glass of champagne," she said. "But this isn't alcohol. This is...wanting you. And needing you."

He picked her up and carried her down the hall—putting her down only when they reached his room. They stepped inside, and he turned on the light. The spacious room was simply furnished with a desk, a chair, an armoire and a king-size bed covered with a white quilted coverlet.

"I never knew I'd been waiting for you," Corey said, burying his face in her hair. "I never knew."

She felt oddly powerful, even as he lowered the shoulder straps of her dress, peeling the bodice down, exposing high, proud breasts to his appraisal. When he bent to kiss the rose-pink nipples, she arched to meet him and threaded her fingers through his hair to hold him to the sweet flesh. She was his equal, though of course her knowledge of lovemaking came not from experience as his did.

Rather, she followed the dictates of her body and her need—which intensified with every new sensation.

She tugged at her dress, wincing as she heard the delicate fabric tear at the back of the waist.

And then she left him staring as she stepped out of her white gown, walking toward the bed with a gait both coltishly awkward and instinctively graceful. She wore nothing but white satin tap pants and stockings held in place by bands of elastic lace. She knelt on the bed, looking over her shoulder to assess his reaction. He leaned against the wall, fully dressed and yet looking somehow more provocative than 007 on his best day. His hand at his elbow drew back his jacket and Robyn was pleased and yet in a very real sense afraid of his sex.

He was hesitating, she knew, at war with himself over making love. By leaving his arms for one instant, she had given the forces of ''No!'' more power. He was afraid of taking advantage of her, she suspected. He thought of her as a mere child. He didn't realize that she was a woman now.

She was a woman, wasn't she?

"Aren't you going to take your clothes off?" she asked.

He swallowed, his Adam's apple bobbing. She lay on her side, displaying her breasts to him.

"No, I won't undress," he said at last. "You're going to do it."

He sauntered to the bed, shrugging out of his tuxedo jacket and waiting for her to do her will. She knelt on the bed, watching the fiery tumult in his eyes as she pulled at the tie, then unbuttoned one and the next stud on his pleated shirt.

She splayed her hands on his unforgivingly muscular chest and felt the drumbeat of his heart, a tribute to her new, magically feminine powers. She pushed aside his shirt and struggled with the belt and buttons and zipper of his pants before giving up.

"Here, I'll do that," Corey said.

It was not until the moment at which he stood, naked and proud before her, that she felt her power over him being exchanged for her surrender. And yet, in the push-pull relationship of their youth, any surrender to his will or his intelligence had wounded her pride.

Being an O'Halleran, she had a lot of pride. Yet now, in this bed, pride meant nothing.

Being made a woman in his arms meant everything. She reached for him and he went to her, then, abruptly tugging away from her embrace, he said, "Robyn, no, baby, we can't. I can't believe I've been such a fool."

"Why can't we?" she asked raggedly.

"I wasn't expecting anything like this to happen," he said. "I don't have any..."

"Don't worry. It's okay," she said boldly. She was close to her period, and besides, what were the odds...her first time...?

"Are you sure?" he asked.

"Sure," she answered with more confidence than she possessed.

She laid her hand on the ridge of his abdominal muscles, not having the boldness to touch—

"You can touch me anywhere," he said softly, almost as a plea. "And I'm going to touch you. Everywhere."

He had the power over her. He set the pace of his touch, and he *did* touch her everywhere, and her hips bucked against him as he held his palm to her pubic mound. Just when she thought she had to beg him to enter her, he pulled her panties— damp with longing—off and tossed them aside. He spread her legs and entered her in a motion gentle, yet swift and sure. There was pain—but only for the briefest moment. Then came the pleasure, the pleasure so intense that she knew she would do anything for him, anything, so that he would make love to her...again and again and again.

So this is what it has come to, she thought in a brief moment of lucidity. Our relationship, once a struggle, is now complete. This is what it has come to…

And then she lost the train of thought as she heard herself cry out, as if from a great distance, his name…once, twice and then again.

"IS IT ALWAYS like that?" Robyn asked, fluffing the pillows and laying her head down contentedly.

"Always? Not always," Corey said. He lay like a sated tiger, with his hands behind his head. "Physically, yes. But emotionally, no. In fact, I think never. Not until this night."

"Have you had a lot of women?"

"Robyn!"

"I'm just asking. It's fine if you have—just so you know you're not having any other women again."

He chuckled. He was startled by her brash confidence, but while he generally lived up to all the expectations of a man of his age, he wondered if it would be possible to ever make love to another woman, when he was absolutely sure he had just lost his heart to Robyn.

So much had changed for him, the world doing a one-eighty, that he wasn't sure what it meant.

"I have to admit I'm stunned. I always thought of you as a tomboy."

For the first time, Robyn didn't bristle.

"I always thought of you as terribly old, terribly arrogant," she said. "But all that's changed now. I want to make love all the time—never do anything else. Just spend every day making love."

Corey sat up.

"Robyn, you know I'm leaving tomorrow."

"For New York. I know. I'll move out there. I could find a college nearby or take a job, one that doesn't have a lot of crazy hours."

"No, Robyn, don't. You're not moving to New York. You're going to do whatever you were going to do before tonight."

Robyn sat up and faced him. And was suddenly aware of her nakedness—a fact that hadn't bothered her two minutes ago, but which now made her hold a sheet up over her breasts.

"But I thought this meant we were together."

"Robyn," he said, taking her face in his hands, "I love you. I really do. And one day, I hope to take this further. To make you my wife. But I can't make that commitment right now. I have a four-year residency in emergency room medicine, starting tomorrow. It's the toughest residency in the toughest New York hospital. Hundred—heck—hundred-and-twenty-hour weeks. No vacation, no holidays, not even Christmas off. I can't be the man I want to be for you. I can't take you on long picnics at the park, I can't rent a cabin for the weekend, I can't take time off to go to your graduation. This can't go anywhere right now."

She jerked out of his embrace.

"Fine," she said, though her heart was breaking. "I guess I misunderstood you, Mr. Chicago's Most Eligible Bachelor. Is this what you tell your other women?"

"Robyn, you're deliberately misunderstanding me now," Corey said, reaching up to stop her as she got out of bed. But she was too quick for him, and already had her panties on when he added, "Baby, you are eighteen years old. A lot can happen to you in the next four years. I'm not going to make you promise me anything, even though one day I think we will marry. And when I'm done with this residency, I will do everything in my power to woo you. But not now. Not now. This is for your own good, Robyn. I'm older and I've seen more of the world than you have and I know..."

But she wasn't listening. She was too numb. Her legs ached with his lovemaking, but while that ache had, moments before, felt delicious, now it just...hurt. She picked up her dress, rued the tiny rip at its back zipper and slipped it over her head. Its handpleats were limp and flat, the lace ribbon wrinkled and worn.

Corey came to her, tugging off a thin gold band he wore on his pinky. He seemed unconcerned about his nakedness, but Robyn kept her eyes firmly planted on his face. Now she regarded their lovemaking as a submission to his will, and she was not a woman who submitted to anyone.

"This is my mother's ring," he said. Mrs. Harte had died when Corey was born, and Corey had worn the ring ever since it had fit on his finger. "I'm giving it to you because I love you."

"But not enough to make any promises," Robyn said crisply. "Not even to say that we're dating. Going steady. Whatever."

"No, I can't do any of that. You can't do any of that, although you don't realize it," he said, slipping the ring onto her middle finger after figuring out that her ring finger was too slim for the ring. "Robyn, I'm trying to be the smart one here."

Tugging her hand out of his grip, Robyn felt the familiar O'Halleran pride rushing through her.

"You always are the smart one," she said. "No, no, you're right. Thanks to your father's generosity, I just came out at the fanciest debutante ball in the country. I have my whole life ahead of me. What's that saying? So many men, so little time?"

Corey closed his eyes.

"Robyn, you're misunderstanding me."

"No, I understand you just fine."

"Please don't leave."

But she had picked up her evening bag and sprinted out the door. He caught up with her at the elevator.

"Don't go," he said. "Let's talk about this."

"There's nothing to talk about," Robyn said.

She gave him a top-to-toe appraisal before entering the elevator.

Two white-gowned debs came out of the elevator on the other side of the hall. They looked at Corey, their mouths widening to perfect round pink *O*s. Corey looked down at his naked chest, his naked abdomen, his naked— The debs giggled behind their hands before gliding down the hallway.

"Hope you remembered to bring your room key," Robyn said, just as the elevator doors closed. She heard an oath and her name and then nothing more.

And she told herself "O'Hallerans never cry" over and over, while she waded through the post-ball crowd in the lobby of the Drake.

She walked up Michigan Avenue to hail a cab, hoping she wouldn't run into any of the other debs. Sitting in the cab on the way back to the Little Village neighborhood where she and her aunt Rose lived, she repeated the mantra over and over.

O'Hallerans never cry. O'Hallerans never cry. O'Hallerans never cry....

She repeated it so often that she believed it, and Aunt Rose found her scant hours later—dry-eyed at the breakfast table with the paper and a cup of coffee. She had carefully put her dress away and changed into a pair of jeans. Corey's ring lay on her dresser.

"Why, is that a picture of you and Corey?" Aunt Rose asked, looking over Robyn's shoulder.

"He's putting on your shoe. Fancy that. Just like a regular Cinderella, you are."

"It's not Cinderella," Robyn said bleakly. "It's Chicago's most eligible bachelor seducing one more woman with his charm."

The telephone rang, and Aunt Rose picked it up. "It's Corey. He's at the airport."

"Tell him I don't want to talk to him. Ever. Again."

Aunt Rose soberly delivered the news. Then she hung up and sat down heavily on the chair next to Robyn's. That's when the tears came, hard and heavy, and Robyn said to her aunt, "I've made a terrible mistake."

ROBYN THOUGHT her mistake had been in making love to him and, perhaps more damaging, innocently believing that making love meant marriage—or at least a romance. Over the next four weeks of Christmas break from school, her feelings softened, so that she could see the wisdom in his words, could feel the love for him as much a part of herself as the dash of freckles across her nose. She even took to wearing his ring around her neck on a thin gold chain. Four years and then perhaps they'd be together—but in the meantime he didn't want her to sacrifice one moment of the pleasures of coming into her adulthood simply because he was in service to his medical training.

It made sense, didn't it?

He was trying to be the older, smarter one.

Even if he was older, but not any smarter.

One day, she'd take his phone calls. One day, she'd accept the flowers that were frequently delivered. One day, she'd open one of the letters from him—and not scribble "return to sender" on the envelope before sticking it back in the mail.

But the true nature of her mistake became clear on the last morning of Christmas break when she awoke strangely queasy. She at first thought it might be her period, starting late, but no. She came into the kitchen for breakfast, stood for a moment by Aunt Rose as she prepared her traditional meal of eggs and sausages. Robyn had always liked the guilty pleasure.

Except *this* morning.

Afterward, Aunt Rose came to the bathroom with a cool, wet towel. "I've been watching you," she said. "It's time to call Corey."

Robyn stared at her aunt with new, terrifying understanding.

"You have a lot to learn," Aunt Rose said, shaking her head.

Robyn looked up from the cold floor that felt so comforting against her face.

"We'll call him now," Aunt Rose added.

Robyn hoisted herself up. "We won't call Corey."

"But we should," Aunt Rose said indignantly. "It's his child."

"No, I won't go to him that way."

"He'll do the right thing, Robyn—I know him that well."

"I know he will do the right thing," Robyn agreed. "And then both of us would pay for our mistake. He's not meant to be a father now."

Aunt Rose shook her head.

"I am so glad that I'm from the O'Neil side of the family—you O'Halleran women are the stubbornest, most prideful, most obstinate—here, take this washcloth. You'll feel better in an hour. And I promise I'll never make sausages in the morning again."

INSIDE THE DRESSER drawer of Ashford Pinksmith III was a receipt. He called his buddy Corey about what to do with it, but Corey was busy, and Ashford was blissfully forgetful about returning messages.

The receipt was pushed farther and farther to the back of the dresser, as socks and shorts and pajamas were stuffed into the drawer.

Three months later, Ashford Pinksmith III didn't even notice when the receipt slipped under the drawer and the Tiffany & Co. salesman stopped leaving voice mail messages.

Chapter Three

Four years later

The twenty-second-floor lobby of Greenough, Hardey & Waite was quiet and subdued: soft classical music was piped in through barely visible speakers on the oak bookshelves; English lithographs of fox-hunting season were displayed on the walls; and intentionally distressed burgundy leather couches and chairs were arranged on faded but no-doubt-about-it expensive Persian rugs.

After announcing herself to the receptionist, Robyn took a seat by the window. She tugged down her periwinkle shantung silk skirt, made a run check on her hose and rubbed for luck the pink-gold Irish Claddagh ring on her left ring finger. Then she pulled an agenda book from her slim black leather envelope-type briefcase.

The agenda, with its precisely written daily schedule, was her vital personal assistant. And it was jam-packed today. This morning she had visited the offices of a bride-to-be who was too busy to come into Aunt Rose's Little Village neighborhood shop for her final fitting. After messengering the dress back to the shop, Robyn had then lunched at the offices of an importer of Egyptian cottons, who was anxious to show her some new acquisitions. Then she'd made a mad dash to Tender Buttons at the corner of Oak and State streets to buy antique mother-of-pearl toggles for a gown that was still in the design stage. She then stopped off at the bank to discuss a loan that would allow her to hire a seamstress as an assistant for Aunt Rose.

Rushed every minute at the behest of her agenda, she had nearly forgotten the mysterious meeting at the upscale law offices. A letter from a senior partner Walter Greenough had been hand-delivered to the shop the day before. He had politely inquired whether she would find it convenient to meet with him at two o'clock this afternoon.

Just like this morning's client, many women who came to White Lace and Promises didn't have the time to spare for three, four and sometimes five fittings Aunt Rose required to make her creations work, but they appreciated the opportunity to purchase couture-quality gowns at reasonable prices. Robyn was quite used to coming downtown to Chicago's Loop to meet these clients at their offices, restaurants and shops. And although she had never received a summons from a male client before, she assumed that a daughter, wife or girlfriend would be introduced in short order.

In addition to her agenda book, her briefcase contained a tape measure, folded tissues to chalk-mark cut-outs from which the dresses would be patterned, sterling silver scissors Aunt Rose had bought her with the money from the first dress they sold and tiny swatches of the finest velvet, satin, silk and lace.

Robyn glanced at the mirror over the couch and touched up her iced-mocha lipstick and smoothed her expertly layered hair. Robyn worked hard to project a professional, sophisticated and—most important—older image. She had taken Aunt Rose's talent with the needle and her own determination and turned what had been a simple tailoring repair shop into a substantial business.

But her fabric suppliers didn't need to know that she was a twenty-three-year-old high school drop-out. Her bank didn't need to know that she spent the wee hours tied up in knots about how to keep up with her bills. Her clients didn't need to know that she had never gone to Paris, Milan or London to find inspiration for White Lace and Promises designs.

Or that on her few days off, Robyn pulled her hair back in a ponytail, wore sneakers and jeans, and didn't even bother with cosmetics.

Or that she was happiest when she and Charlie could slip away to the park for a few hours.

Robyn looked beyond her own image to the back of the man standing at the receptionist's curved desk. He was dark-haired, tall, broadly muscular and wore a black suit cut in the most flattering European style.

She caught herself staring at his reflection…four years ago, she had thought she'd seen Corey in every man at every street corner, on the street, in every restaurant. And then the men she studied would turn around and be someone who wasn't Corey…reopening the wound on her heart.

She had only slowly come to the realization that the folly of that debutante night, while producing the single greatest blessing of her life, had been a wake-up call on being a grown-up.

And she had marched right down the path of responsibility.

While her girlfriends in the neighborhood had been partying late at night, she'd been soothing a colicky baby to sleep. While her friends had spent spring break in Florida, she'd been writing business plans to present to the bank. While her girlfriends had dated the dangerously handsome guys who would eventually break their hearts, Robyn had been having coffee once every two weeks with her accountant.

A month after Charlie was born, Robyn had put a rubber band around her wrist and snapped it hard every time she thought of Corey. Her wrist ended up bruised by the end of just a week, but she was pretty much cured.

Her mother had put raising her daughter ahead of everything in her life—even her love for the older Dr. Harte. And so it would always be for Robyn. Charlie would come first.

She glanced down at the Claddagh ring on her finger—it symbolized a new beginning to her life, one that would reinforce values of responsibility, hard work, patience and persistence.

A single mother needed all of that—and it would help if there were thirty hours in every day.

Odd that now, in a new client's office, she'd think of Corey again. Just the dark hair, the cut of that man's suit...the muscles...

She looked back from the mirror and that's when time and breath stopped.

"Oh, my gosh," she whispered, closing her eyes. But she jerked up her head as he strode over to the couch. She tried to remember what pleasantry she had thought she would say to him if they ever perchance crossed paths—but she had long since trained herself out of the habit of daydreaming about a chance meeting. "Corey Harte, how...how very nice to see you."

Nice? It wasn't nice. It was disconcerting. It was discombobulating. It was like tumbling out of a plane without a parachute.

"It's been a long time, Robyn," he agreed neutrally. "How are you?" He seemed distracted, hardly thrilled to see her.

She stood up, noting with some pride that the high-heeled pumps she wore gave her enough height to meet his...at least his chin. She held out her right hand and gave his a firm, businesslike shake.

"I'm doing all right," she said, her voice honey-smooth professionalism. "How about you?"

"You didn't hear?"

"No. What?"

A flicker of grief passed over his face.

"My father died last week."

He caught her arm as she momentarily lost her balance.

"How terrible," she said, putting her arms out to his broad shoulders. "I'm so sorry. How did it happen?"

He didn't respond. She felt hurt—but realized that she had long since forfeited her right to give him comfort. After all, he thought she had dumped him. She'd refused every contact until several months before Charlie's birth, when she'd made Aunt Rose tell him she was in college and happily dating another man. End of phone calls, end of flowers, end of letters—end of Corey.

"It was in his sleep," Corey said finally. "A heart attack. He had had high blood pressure, but we never thought it was that serious."

"Will there be any kind of memorial service?"

Robyn asked, knowing that if Dr. Harte had died last week, she had probably missed the funeral. "I'd like to go. That is, if you wouldn't mind. I mean I haven't talked to him since…"

"You always had a soft spot for the old man," Corey said, and Robyn realized that he was going to act as if nothing had ever happened between them on the night of the ball. Perhaps that was for the best…

"He was very good to me."

"There isn't a memorial, but I spread his ashes on Lake Michigan as he requested. And tomorrow night there's a benefit for the hospital. He wanted to give the hospital the Harte house so that families could stay someplace comfortable while their children were being treated."

He wearily sat down on the couch and patted the seat beside him.

"So, what about you? You look like a regular businesswoman," he said admiringly. "What are you up to?"

"White Lace and Promises," she said, proudly pulling out a business card from her purse. She tugged her skirt down over her knees.

He dutifully studied the ecru card with its lace border.

"You make dresses?"

"Aunt Rose makes them. I take care of everything else. And there's a lot of everything else. Importing the fabrics, meeting with clients, developing advertising and keeping an eye on finances. We still live in the apartment over the shop.''

''What are you doing here?'' he asked, returning her card.

''I'm seeing a new client—Walter Greenough.''

Corey did a double take.

''I never knew Walter wore dresses.''

''I don't know that he does. Maybe he wants to surprise his wife with a new gown.''

''He doesn't have a wife.''

''Maybe he has a girlfriend.''

Corey shook his head.

He gave her a long, hard look. ''You know, Robyn, you look wonderful. Really wonderful. You've become a very beautiful woman.''

''Thank you,'' she said. ''Are you going back to New York soon?''

''I finished my residency,'' he said, his voice catching. ''Northwestern offered me their trauma-care unit. They want me to hire the doctors I want to work with, the nurses I need, the support staff. It's a big undertaking, but at least I'm back in Chicago. Look…I know we didn't part on the best of terms, but maybe we could get together some-time.''

''Oh, I don't know. Perhaps.'' Then she added quickly and decisively, ''But I should warn you I'm very busy these days.''

It was a relief when the receptionist announced

that Mr. Greenough was prepared to see them.

Both of them.

WALTER GREENOUGH was a highly respected attorney who specialized in taking care of wealthy people and their money. The walls of his office were covered with awards and certificates from professional associations, as well as two degrees from Harvard. The coffee table—placed away from his desk for those putting-his-clients-at-ease conversations—was littered with Limoges collectibles.

Yet, for all his accomplishment and professional acclaim, Walter Greenough was, from the top of his six-foot frame to the bottom of his wingtips, a virtual fourteen-year-old. His wrists stuck out of his Armani suit as if he were in the midst of a growth spurt. His gray hair fell in front of his face as though he had put off the trip to the barber. He slouched in his leather desk chair—anyone observing him knew he'd never listened to his mother when she'd told him to sit up straight.

"Hey," he said, with the inflection of a teen inviting cohorts to join him at a video-game parlor. "Find a seat anywhere."

Robyn sat on a tufted, green velvet couch and Corey sat across from her on a Lindberg-style leather chair.

"If this is about a dress," Robyn began.

Walter leaned over his desk, working a paper clip sculpture in his hand.

"A dress?"

"Yes, do you want a dress?"

"God, no, I usually wear pants."

"Then why did you invite me here?"

"You're both here about Dr. Harte's will," Walter said.

Robyn shook her head. "I don't want to hear this...."

"I'm sure my father wanted to leave you something," Corey said pleasantly. "He was always very fond of you. And your mother, too."

"Please, Miss O'Halleran," Walter said. "It's required that you be present when I do this."

Robyn crossed her legs and settled in.

While Walter read through the preliminary wherefores and heretofores that might as well have been in semaphore language, Robyn thought about the elder Dr. Harte. She truly was shocked by his death—he often called himself a simple country doctor, but his medical inventions had saved many lives and the patents had given him enormous wealth—he was meant to live forever, if only because the work he did was so desperately needed.

She had never communicated with him after sending a letter thanking him for the chance to go to the cotillion ball and for giving her a good start in life. Although she had expected and dreaded some uncomfortable questions, he had quietly honored her estrangement and had merely sent a short note telling her that he was proud of her and would always be available to see her if she chose.

She wondered if he would have wanted to see Charlie, to know that his only son had a son.

Holding a secret was hard, especially when the man who was most affected by it was seated so close to her. She wondered if she should tell him. Tell him now. Tell him that he had a link to the next generation, and in a way compensate him for losing his link to the one before him.

"Ms. O'Halleran," Walter Greenough said. "I know this is tremendously boring legal mumbo-jumbo, but during this part you should listen very carefully."

Party of the first part. In perpetuity. The trustee shall hold all assets with remainder to be determined.

Couldn't lawyers speak English?

Her thoughts drifted as Walter continued to read, the sentences running longer and longer, the phrases grander and more eloquent, the syllable count on each word rising rapidly.

If Dr. Harte left her any money, she couldn't possibly accept. But perhaps she could use it to expand the White Lace and Promises program of making white prom gowns for inner-city high school girls too poor to buy their own. The program had worked the past two years—although designing and sewing over a hundred formal gowns was a massive undertaking.

In fact, she was just thinking about how, regardless of what she learned in this office today, she should call the principal of the high school to find out how many girls would be needing prom dresses this coming June.

She looked up and paid attention when she noticed that the atmosphere of the room had turned most decidedly chilly.

Pulling her shantung jacket closer around her, she gaped at Corey, who had swept aside the Limoges collectibles and put his elbows down on the coffee table so that he could scrutinize her.

Really scrutinize her.

And he had an expression on his face nearly exactly matching the glare he had given her when she threw water balloons from the roof of the Harte house—nailing his date for the high school prom.

"What's wrong?" she asked.

"You."

"What'd I do?"

"You had a son. My son."

"Oh, Corey."

"I guess you forgot to mention that, when we met in the lobby—" his voice rose "—or any other time in the past four years."

Furious. Robyn opened her mouth, closed it, looked at the gawky lawyer behind his desk and then back at Corey. He was furious.

When confronted with his sopping wet prom date, Robyn had explained that she had never meant to hit anybody. An accident, she had said.

Corey had ordered her to apologize. And he had

been angry. Very angry. But right now he looked furious. And she couldn't blame him.

"Corey is the trustee for your child," Walter explained. "And the doctor left half of his estate to your son."

"What? How did he know?" Robyn asked.

"Dr. Harte discovered you had given birth when one of his colleagues at the neighborhood hospital you delivered at told him. He said he didn't contact you because he wanted to respect your choices."

Robyn gulped, realizing the pain that Dr. Harte must have experienced, knowing that a grandson lived, yet never getting to be with him, never holding him.

"The duties of a trustee," Walter said, clearing his throat, "are to manage the trust for the benefit of the child. So Corey's responsibilities to your son as a trustee are to invest assets, manage funds and make disbursements for—"

"Trustee, hell, I'm his father!" Corey said. He jabbed a finger toward Robyn. "You had my baby. You didn't even tell me!"

Robyn jumped to her feet, about to defend her actions. But he gave her no time to speak.

"You kept my child from me!"

"I did it for your own good. You couldn't have been a father. You didn't have time. You'd made it clear you didn't have time...for me...for anything."

They stood toe-to-toe, and he had a good six

inches on her, even in heels, but what she didn't have in height she made up for in outrage. She had saved him from the consequences of their love-making—consequences that would have put him off his certain track of success.

She had had four years to think about what the debutante ball had meant to her...and to him. And she knew as surely as she knew brides wore white to weddings and tulle wholesaled for $3.99 a yard that Corey had regarded their lovemaking as a one-night stand—he had not meant it to be more.

And she had made sure it wasn't more because she loved him enough to let him go.

He had no right to—

But she always knew this day would come—she just thought it would be later...and quieter...and more private.

"I know you would have wanted to know," she said. "And I was going to tell you."

"When?"

She ducked her head.

"I don't know—but I wanted you to get through your residency, establish yourself as a doctor and maybe settle down."

"Settle down?"

She jerked her head back up.

"I read the papers. You're the one supposed to be going out with movie stars...."

"It was just once. We went to an opera, and she fell in love with the tenor."

"Models..."

"Their press agents feed the media that stuff so they'll stay in the spotlight."

"And that princess from—"

"That was one night and I was asked to escort her to the fund-raiser for the hospital. They gave me the night off."

"You were photographed the next morning coming out of her hotel room!"

"I fell asleep on her couch while she was taking off her jewelry for the security staff. You've certainly been keeping up with my life."

"It's tough not to, when you're one of the most eligible bachelors in Chicago *and* New York. I can't read a newspaper without seeing your picture."

"It's how the press makes their money. I am a doctor first—and a bachelor second."

He sat down.

"Now I'm a dad." His voice drained of anger. "Wow. I'm a dad. Tell me...what's he like?"

Robyn sat down and tugged at her jacket.

"You're a little shell-shocked."

"A lot," Walter said, observing them over his bifocals. "Corey, do you need a drink?"

"No, I'm fine," Corey said. "I'm just... surprised. It's going to take me a few minutes to get used to the idea."

"Take all the time you want," Walter offered.

Corey took a deep breath.

"There was no man," he said. "When Aunt Rose told me to stop trying to see you, she said you had found someone. But there wasn't anybody, was there?"

Robyn looked down.

"She said you were having so much fun in college with your new boyfriend."

Robyn pulled on a thread that was hanging from the hem of her skirt.

"There was no man and no college and no 'girls just wanna have fun.'"

"No, there wasn't."

"You weren't ready, either, were you?"

"No."

"I'm ready now."

"I don't think you're ready to be a dad," she said. "It's a big shock hearing about this—especially this way. And I apologize for that. But you don't have the time or energy for being a dad. Not a real dad."

"No, I'm ready," Corey said. "I'm ready to be a dad. In fact, the more I think about it, the more I like it. It's a weird feeling being so mad at you for not telling me about this earlier, and at the same time I'm...well, happy to be a father. So...what's his name?"

"Charlie."

"Charlie. Whose eyes does he have?"

"Yours. Blue as the sky."

"Hair?" Corey asked softly.

"Dark chocolate brown."

"Healthy?"

"Absolutely," Robyn said, a smidgen of maternal pride creeping into her voice.

"Walking? Talking?"

"Right on schedule."

"When do I see him?"

Robyn took a deep breath. She knew this day would come, but she had always thought she would have the luxury of being in control. Of being the one to tell him how things would be. She knew she would be generous. Charlie deserved a father. Corey deserved his son. It was just that Corey couldn't handle all the responsibilities of fatherhood....

"Here," she said. She opened her wallet and pulled out a snapshot.

Corey took the picture. He stared silently. His jaw moved slightly and then he closed his eyes. He put the picture in his suit jacket pocket and sat in the armchair.

"Hey, that's my—"

His eyes popped open, and she knew she had hit his limit.

"I'd like you to have that picture," she amended. "My gift."

"Thank you," he said with strained courtliness. "And when do I get an introduction?"

"I'll have to prepare him and Aunt Rose for this."

His smile was as indulgent as a pat on the head.

"Today, Robyn. I'll help you prepare them for the shock. And since we're going to be together a lot in the next eighteen years, let's talk fatherhood."

"You can visit him whenever you want to. Dinners, afternoons at the park," Robyn said, struggling for control. "Going to museums, even an overnight visit when he's a little older. Anything that can fit into your busy schedule. And my business schedule. And Charlie's schedule."

"Forget that stuff, Robyn," Corey said calmly. "I'm going to be a father to him in every way. I'm living with Charlie. Starting today."

Unconcerned with her sputtering reply, Corey leaned back in his plushly cushioned chair and put his hands behind his head.

"Walter, get the judge. Robyn and I are getting hitched."

"Now?" Walter asked.

"By the end of business hours today."

Walter, who had made a good living getting his clients what they wanted when they wanted it, said he'd make a few phone calls. He walked out of the office, and Robyn dearly wished she could have followed him.

She had spent the last four years getting her world in order, and Corey looked as though he could destroy all of it in just a matter of hours.

"I can't marry you," she said.

He stood up, coming over to her and she was forced to tilt her head back to meet his gaze.

"We'll work something out, but I can't marry you," she said, leaning back.

He didn't speak, merely reached out to trail his fingers along her collarbone. She hadn't been touched in a long, long time, and without meaning to, she closed her eyes and sighed...even as a voice inside her head screamed "Mistake!"

His fingers drifted to the swell of her breasts, rounder and fuller in motherhood. A memory of his scent, citrus and musk—was it real? Would it make her forget four years? She instinctively reared up to meet his hand and then jerked upright.

She needn't have bothered.

Caressing her wasn't his intention. Instead, he pulled the slender gold chain from beneath her ice pink silk shell. Robyn's eyes popped open, she looked down at the ring he held.

His ring. His mother's ring.

"We're getting married, Robyn," he said. "Because we should. We have a son. We owe it to him. This ring will do nicely. I'm glad you kept it."

He undid the chain, keeping the ring. The chain slithered down her clothes, dropping onto the carpet.

He took her left hand.

"Robyn, we will marry and we will make this work because—"

His cheeks paled. His eyes widened, and then closed.

He swore, expelling all the air in his lungs, and his shoulders dropped.

"Corey, I should have warned you."

"Yes, you should have."

He put his mother's ring in his suit jacket pocket and studied the ring she wore on her left ring finger.

Chapter Four

"Are you married?"

She shook her head.

"Engaged?"

"No."

"Living with someone?"

"I'm not living with anyone. Just Aunt Rose and Charlie."

"Then, what's this?"

Robyn took a deep breath, trying to figure out the best way to explain Bob.

Bob, the man who was her answer to growing up.

Bob, the anchor that had brought her ship to calm waters.

"I'm going to be engaged."

"Going to be, but not yet?"

She nodded.

"What is this ring for? Is it like going steady or getting pinned?"

"My fiancé—"

"Don't call him that if he's not one."

"Bob. That's his name. My boyfriend, Bob," she said, choosing to ignore the fleeting look of disgust that flickered across Corey's face. "Bob gave me this ring last month as a token of his intentions. And he flew to Ireland yesterday to ask his mother's permission before officially asking me to be his bride."

The expression on Corey's face told her exactly what he thought of men who asked their mother's permission to marry. She plowed on.

"I know it sounds crazy. But I think it's kind of sweet. She's very old-fashioned, and he knew she'd want to be consulted though he's still going to marry me even if she doesn't approve."

"Why wouldn't she approve?"

"I'm an unwed mother," Robyn pointed out tartly. "For some people, there's a lot to disapprove."

"And his mother's approval or disapproval means that much?"

"Yes."

Corey stretched and yawned. Bob was dismissed as far as he was concerned.

"Marry me and you're not an unwed mother anymore."

"If I marry you I can't marry Bob."

For the first time since he saw the ring, he smiled. "That's the beauty part of the plan."

"I'm not marrying you. I'm marrying Bob. He is a wonderful man."

"He's not a man. He's a mouse. And you don't love him. You can't love him."

"I do. We have a lot of shared interests and mutual respect and the same work ethic," she said, adding quickly as Corey made a face. "He really loves me."

"I'm not having that man raise my son."

"Are you just going to disapprove of everything about him?"

"If a man's old enough to marry, he doesn't need his parents' permission." He paced. "And shared interests, respect and work ethic...that isn't why you get married."

"Look, you're in shock, Corey, you're not thinking straight."

"Oh, I'm thinking just fine. I know I want Bob out of the picture. I also know he's easy to dispose of."

"Easy?"

"He probably scares easy. And I'm in the mood to scare him."

"Don't you lay a hand on him."

"I won't have to. I'll speak sternly."

"I am marrying him!"

"Robyn, you've always been headstrong, but here's where it stops. You call Bob and tell him the wedding's off. His mother will be relieved, and we don't need him making life more complicated than it already is. Besides, he can't give you what you want, and he can't give Charlie what he needs.''

"And just what it is that I want and Charlie needs?"

"Charlie needs a dad, a *man* in his life, and you…" He leaned forward and gave her the once-over. Twice. She did a quick button check on her blouse. "You need a man. A *real* man. A man who can make love to you. All—" his lips touched her ear "—night—" his breath sent a shiver of pleasure all the way down her back "—long."

"I'll let you see Charlie whenever you want," Robyn snapped, pulling up sharply and crossing her legs tightly. "We can work out a custody schedule."

Corey shrugged as if he were a cat and this mouse could be had whenever he chose.

"I want to be Charlie's father all the time. When I wake up in the morning. Last thing before I go to sleep. I want to see his reflection in the mirror when I'm shaving. I want to have him wake me up when there are monsters under his bed in the middle of the night. I want to be his all-the-time daddy. And that makes me your all-the-time man."

"I think you're being very presumptuous," Robyn said, rising to her feet. "I won't marry you."

"Okay, we can live together in sin, but you have

to be the one to tell him when he's old enough why you wouldn't marry his dad.''

"I won't live in sin—with you or any other man. Corey, having a child together doesn't mean that we have a relationship. Sinful or marital.''

"It's better for our son to have two parents,'' Corey said, tugging her hand.

Robyn gave him a withering stare.

"It's better for our son to know that you don't marry for any other reason than love. Because only love will make a marriage last. And that's the one word you haven't mentioned. Not once.''

"What about Bob. Do you call that love?''

Robyn was silent. "Look, Corey, I give you credit for trying to do the right thing,'' she said. "We'll work something out...something where you can see him and be part of his life. But leave marriage out of it.''

"If I told you I loved you right now, you wouldn't believe me, would you?''

"No,'' she said, shaking her head. "You told me four years ago that you were trying to be the smart one. Now it's my turn. It's unwise, completely stupid, in fact, for us to get married.''

"Like it or not, wise or foolish, we're doing it,'' he said firmly.

Walter opened the office door and poked his head in.

"Hey, buddy, the judge is here,'' he said.

With his unbuttoned black robe flapping behind

him, a stocky gentleman in a three-piece suit strode into the office.

"Robyn, let me introduce Judge Campbell," Corey said, rising to his feet. "He was a friend of my father's."

Taking the length of the office in four broad strides, Judge Campbell grabbed Robyn's hand between his own and shook...hard. He was used to running unopposed in the judicial elections, but he would have relished the chance to campaign.

"Glad to meet you!" he boomed. "So you're the lucky gal who's finally brought Chicago's most eligible bachelor to the altar!"

Robyn smiled faintly. She wondered how she'd break it to the judge that there wasn't going to be a wedding, but it was tough to get a word in edgewise as the judge outlined the traffic obstacles he had surmounted on his way to meet them.

"So where's the license?" he demanded, abruptly cutting off his own story.

"I sent a messenger over to the county clerk's office to pick up the forms, and there's a lab technician from Corey's outpatient clinic here with the blood test kit," Walter said. He handed Robyn a limp, dripping bouquet of pink tulips. "I took these from a vase on my secretary's desk."

"Put them back in water," the judge said, pulling a slim, leather appointment book from within the voluminous folds of his robe. "I can come back tomorrow. Say three-ish?"

"Why not right now?" Corey asked.

"The twenty-four hour waiting period is mandatory in Illinois," the judge explained, wagging a finger at Corey. "It's to stop impetuous youths from doing something they might regret. Frankly, I'm a little annoyed to be pulled out of court for this, but your father and I went way back, and I'll let you off with just a reprimand. What's the big rush, anyway?"

He regarded Robyn's smooth figure out of the corner of his eye.

"It's not like that," Corey said. "The baby's already born."

"Then if you waited this long you could wait long enough to do it the old-fashioned way."

"Old-fashioned way?" Corey asked.

"Flowers, champagne, cake, music, rice."

"I'm sorry, Your Honor," Robyn said. "But we're not getting married. At all."

The judge looked quite curiously at Robyn.

"She'll change her mind," Corey said.

"Son, I don't want to see you do something foolish," Judge Campbell said, putting his agenda back in his suit jacket pocket. "Take the next few days and we'll talk."

"He's in shock," Robyn said. "He'll come to his senses in a day or two."

"Saturday," Corey said.

"Okay, I'll pencil you in for Saturday." Judge Campbell wrote in his appointment book. "I'll either officiate at your wedding or you'll call me and tell me it's not happening. Either way, I've got to head back to traffic court. Drivers these days, you can't imagine!''

''Saturday it is,'' Corey said firmly.

''Saturday is when my fiancé returns from Ireland,'' Robyn said, putting the tulips on the table.

The judge shook his head.

''Corey, don't pull this kind of prank on me.''

''It's not a prank. We're getting married.''

''Uh, Judge Campbell, maybe I could explain the matrimonial problems,'' Walter said. ''As it happens, I've got to be in court in a half hour. We'll share a cab and I'll explain everything.''

''Thanks, Walter. Your Honor, see you Saturday,'' Corey said. He snatched Robyn's hand.

''Where are we going?'' she demanded, grabbing her briefcase as they hurtled past the couch.

''We're going to meet my son and plan our wedding.''

''Corey, we're not getting married.''

But his grip was strong and his will even stronger. Robyn had no doubt that if she didn't match him, stride for stride, down the long hallway, he would throw her over his shoulder and carry her.

''Hi, Jamal,'' Corey said to a white-coated black man who stood waiting at the receptionist's desk. ''Robyn, this is Jamal from my clinic. Roll up your sleeve.''

"Forget it," Robyn said.

"There's a blood test requirement in this state."

"No use going against the doctor when he's got his mind set on something," Jamal advised.

"Robyn, take off your suit jacket and roll up your sleeve."

"My fiancé's coming back Saturday and I'm not marrying—"

In one swift motion, Corey had her silk shantung sleeve rolled up, the tourniquet on and had poked her.

"Ouch!"

"Got the vein. First shot. I work with kids," Corey explained, putting a stopper on the vial and starting a second. "I can get blood work from the squirmiest. And you're definitely one of the squirmiest. Put some tape on that, wouldja, Jamal?"

"WEDDINGS ARE so-o-o-o wonderful," gushed the woman wearing a tulle skirt and a bustier. "And so romantic. Don't you think?"

"I totally agree," Corey said. He glanced out from behind a copy of *Insurance Today* and put a gold-headed pin from the sewing kit onto the hand that reached out from under the skirt. He wondered if he could just take that Claddagh ring off her finger, then decided that Robyn was going to be his soon enough—he didn't need to use force. "We're getting married on Saturday."

"Really?" the bride giggled. "That's so-o-o-o cool!"

"Stop moving," Robyn said sharply, her head emerging from under the voluminous tulle. "I can't get your hem pinned if you don't stand still."

Chastened, the bride-to-be stood poker straight on top of the marble coffee table. The trio were in the offices of the president of a major Chicago insurance firm. The president had graciously allowed his secretary the office after she had stood ready for her fitting—on her desk in her cubicle without a hint of modesty or clothing.

Robyn had wanted to cancel the appointment, since the reappearance of Corey had made her fingers shaky and shattered her sense of judgment, but the waiting list for custom-made wedding dresses from White Lace and Promises was two months, and Robyn hated to disappoint a client. The tulle slip had been messengered to the bride two weeks before for her to approve, and unfortunately the work of creating the rest of the gown was a week behind schedule. And when Robyn told Corey she would meet him later, he'd told her there was no way he was letting go of her until he met his son.

"Where is your ceremony being held?" the woman on the coffee table asked, pirouetting to let Robyn get a sense of how wide the skirt would flounce.

"We haven't decided," Corey said. He put *In-*

surance Today back on the coffee table and picked up the latest issue of *Mutual Annuities Journal.*

"That's awfully short notice. You'll never get a decent hotel or restaurant."

"We'll get married at my house. It's going to be a small wedding."

"Who are you using as a caterer?"

Robyn muttered from beneath the skirt.

"Hadn't thought of that," Corey said. "Catering is a good idea, though. People always like food."

"*We're* using Entre Vous. Preston True, the chef, is a genius. What are you doing about flowers?"

"Do you know a good florist?"

The grumbling from under the skirt was getting louder.

"What did you say, darling?" Corey said amiably.

"I said there isn't going to be a wedding," Robyn stated, pulling herself up from her knees.

Her hair was wildly tousled, just the way he remembered it—none of this prim-and-proper stuff. Her face was pink, reminding him of the blush she wore four years ago. He wouldn't mind a kiss. He glanced up at the secretary.

Couldn't kiss Robyn here.

Not the right atmosphere with a half-naked woman in a tutu gawking at you. Still, Corey felt okay. He knew it would happen soon.

Robyn held up the tape measure. "I need to take

measurements from the waist up. Raise your arms over your head.''

''Robyn, I know I made a mistake not marrying you four years ago,'' Corey said, picking another pin out of the kit. ''But I'm making up for lost time now. And our son deserves a father. And a mother. And a home. Can't we act like adults about this?''

''I'm acting like an adult,'' Robyn said. ''You're in a state of shock.''

''I'm over the shock. I'm even over the being mad that you didn't tell me. I want to marry you. I look at you now and I remember what we had that night.''

''A bad case of lust, if I remember.''

The bride-to-be looked from one to the other.

Corey picked up *Whole Term Tribune* and snapped it open.

''I'm not marrying a man who's doing it out of obligation or because he's doing the honorable thing,'' Robyn said, taking the waist measurement. ''When I marry, it's got to be for love. Like when I marry Bob.''

''Forget Bob. I'm the one who loves you,'' Corey said, looking up from his magazine. ''I've always loved you. From the day your mother first came to work for us—you were just six years old. I loved you then and I love you now.''

''Maybe as a friend, but not as a wife,'' Robyn countered. She looked up at her client. ''Would you marry a man who's putting a ring on your finger only because he thinks it's the right thing to do?''

''No, of course not,'' the bride-to-be said, shaking her head so vehemently her curls pulled away from her headband.

''What if he was the father of your child?'' Corey asked.

''I don't know what I'd do then.''

''Does your fiancé love you?'' Corey asked.

''Corey, butt out,'' Robyn said.

''No, I want to know. Miss, does your fiancé love you?''

''Of course.''

''How do you know? I mean, how does a man persuade a woman that he does love her?''

''My Norman says 'likewise' whenever I say I love you,'' the bride-to-be said. ''But now that you mention it, I always have to say it first. I wonder if that means Norman doesn't love me?''

She looked at Corey and at Robyn. Corey trained his eyes on the opening paragraph of an article on whole-term insurance regulations in the state of Florida. It was boring as all get-out, but better than meeting Norman's fiancée's eye. Robyn wrote down two measurements on the pattern sheet.

''I'm sure Norman loves you,'' Robyn said quietly. ''Could I get you to turn around so I can measure your back?''

"I don't think 'likewise' counts," Corey said from behind the cover of his magazine. "It's what guys say when they want to change the topic."

"Corey," Robyn warned.

"It's true. I've heard the talk in the doctor's locker room at the hospital. 'Likewise' means let's talk about something else."

"Maybe you're right," the bride-to-be said, unsnapping her waistband. Corey shoved his head into the magazine as her skirt hit the floor.

"Corey, stop talking about getting married!" Robyn ordered. "Why can't we just see how things work out between us as parents?"

"Because your stupid almost fiancé, Bob, is coming home on Saturday with a permission slip pinned to his jacket!" he roared.

Chapter Five

It might be a Tuesday. It might be three o'clock in the afternoon. Bank presidents, law-firm partners and office managers might still consider it working hours, but it was the first sunny April afternoon, and Chicagoans are smart enough to take advantage of a treasure like that. Michigan Avenue was throbbing—shoppers with bulging twine-handled bags, students with backpacks and attitude, hooky-playing workers with their suit jackets slung over their shoulders.

When Robyn and Corey stepped out onto the sidewalk, they competed with boom boxes, blaring horns and the groan of a bus sideswiping the curb.

Despite the hustle and bustle, Robyn's words carried. "You lost me a client!"

"I'm sorry."

"And we just broke up a relationship!"

"It wasn't me that did that."

"You didn't have to tell her that 'likewise' is male talk for 'I really don't.'"

"She had to find out sometime—better before the wedding than after." He took her elbow.

"And where are we going now?" she demanded.

"I'm getting us a cab and we're going home," he said, lifting his hand high to hail a cab. "I've waited long enough to meet my son."

He climbed into the cab behind her and gave the Little Village address to the driver. Then he settled back in the seat, his knees propped up against the back of the passenger seat.

"Corey, we need to prepare Aunt Rose and Charlie. We should take it slow."

"I know, but I waited patiently while you finished up with that client."

Robyn glared.

"All right, you win," Corey said. "Cabbie, we'll be going to 1248 Astor Street."

"What's that?" Robyn asked suspiciously.

"My new house. Just bought it a couple of months ago. I figure we should plan on twenty-four hours. I don't have any patients scheduled, but you might want to call Aunt Rose and tell her where you'll be."

"Twenty-four hours for what?"

"Twenty-four hours of making love. I figure that's how long it will take for me to make love to you so that you're hopelessly, senselessly, wonderfully incapable of resisting my marriage proposal."

Robyn reared up and shrieked. "You think that if you make love to me, I'm going to lose all reason, perspective and rationality, and I'm going to want to marry you?"

"Yup."

"Of all the arrogant, conceited, pigheaded..."

"Making love will make you fall in love with me—all over again."

"Autocratic, sure-of-yourself—"

"Worked once. It'll work again."

"Cabbie, stop right here!" she howled. "I'm going home!"

"Me, too," Corey said amiably. "Why don't we take a cab together?"

The cab came to an on-a-dime stop, sending Robyn tumbling onto Corey's lap. Horns honked. The driver behind them shoved his head out the window and cursed. A cop directing traffic at the intersection whistled and jabbed his gloved hand accusingly at the cabbie.

"Oh-h-h, that feels nice, Robyn," Corey purred, cupping her buttocks with his hands.

She couldn't have gotten off him faster if he had been a stove with all its burners running.

She jerked primly at her skirt, clutched her blouse where a button had opened, and glared at him.

"Astor Street, please," Corey directed the cabbie.

"Little Village, please," Robyn countered from

behind clenched teeth. "This isn't about sex. It's about responsibility."

"This has everything to do with sex."

"I don't give a damn about your sex life!" snarled the cabbie. He jerked his head back toward them. "Little Village or Astor Street? Tell me now, and then both of ya shut your traps for the whole ride."

"Little Village, please," Robyn said meekly. "If it wouldn't be too much trouble."

"Certainly, miss, no trouble at all," the cabbie said. And he tapped a nonexistent cap, gave a you-should-know-better look to Corey and turned his attention, body and soul to his chosen profession.

Traffic was tight at the bottleneck of Michigan, Oak and Lake Shore Drive. The cab hadn't gone two blocks before Corey leaned close to her and whispered.

"Robyn, we did her a favor." His breath softly caressed her neck. "Their relationship wouldn't have lasted. Norman didn't love her."

Robyn looked to the cabbie for a reprimand. It wasn't coming.

"You don't love me," she whispered back. "So by your own logic, I shouldn't marry you."

"You can say that all you want," he whispered, his lips touching her flesh, "but marriage between us is a certainty. In fact, I predict you will marry me on Saturday and that you'll do it willingly."

She slid a half inch toward the window and out of his reach.

"I'll meet Bob at the airport on Saturday," she said, "and you and I will work out some method of coparenting."

He flashed all his fingers once and then eight fingers a second time.

"What does that mean?" she mouthed, glancing at the cabbie once to make sure they weren't in for a second scolding.

"Eighteen years before Charlie's out of college," Corey murmured silkily. "And I'll be his father for every one of them and forever. We can either do it my way or..."

"Or what?"

"Or we can fight every step of the way. You always were a fighter." He made a fist and chucked her on the chin.

"You always were a dictator."

"Is that what you've told him about me?"

"I haven't told him anything. He's only three years old. He doesn't ask questions about having a dad."

"Now he'll have one," he said, twining his fingers through hers. "Just one."

Robyn tugged hard at her hand, but he didn't give an inch.

"I'm hearing some noise back there," the cabbie warned. "And if I let you off here, on Lake Shore Drive, you're gonna have a long walk.

Whether you're going to Little Village *or* the den of iniquity.''

She tugged again, but Corey held fast. She mouthed a rebuke. He shrugged. She strained against him until her hand turned purple, and then she gave up.

Although Corey had felt angry, truly red-hot angry, when he had first learned of his child, he now could not conjure up that emotion. Instead, as he studied her profile with its pugnacious tilt to the chin, he wondered at the woman who, however wrongly, had thought she must carry the burden of motherhood alone in order to protect him.

He thought of all the experiences that she had missed in her life, things that he, in his oblivious state, had assumed she'd been doing. The hard work of college. The nights in the library. The parties thrown to relieve the pressures of exam week. Dating. Travel. Movies. Restaurants. All things he could not have shared with her.

In fact, during his residency he had often flipped through the movie section of the *New York Times* at the nursing station amazed at how much he missed. He couldn't name an Oscar-winning actor or actress from the past four years. Couldn't name a single prime-time television show. Didn't know who was pitching for the Chicago Cubs he had grown up cheering for. Didn't care who was pitching for New York.

And he had thought he was saving her from this

isolation, when she'd been the one who had made the sacrifices...and reaped the rewards of parenthood.

He had thought he was the wise one.

Well, now he would put things to right.

He craned his neck over the seat as they reached Addison Street.

"Stop here!" he ordered when he saw the White Lace and Promises sign. In front of the shop was a familiar, stout woman in a pink floral sundress. Her auburn hair was peppered with gray, which Corey didn't remember. Her gait was a little slower than he recalled.

But she carried her age with dignity and a regal pride as she pushed a single-seat stroller along the sidewalk.

"No, Corey, we should talk to her first," Robyn said. "Prepare her."

After throwing a twenty-dollar bill on the front seat, Corey yanked on the door handle just as the driver pulled up to the curb. He bounded up the sidewalk.

"Why, Corey, I knew you'd come back," the old woman said in a rich Irish brogue that twenty years in "the new country" hadn't softened. "I expect you'll be wanting to meet your son."

Corey glanced back at the taxi from which Robyn was just emerging.

"This isn't a shock?"

"Not at all. I've been waiting four years for

this," Aunt Rose said. "I wake up every morning thinkin' I wouldna be surprised to see you today. Introduce yourself to your son."

He crouched in front of the stroller, meeting the solemn saucer-wide eyes of a dark-haired three-year-old in a blue-and-green-striped T-shirt and matching shorts.

"Corey, this is Charlie. Charlie, say hello to your da," said Aunt Rose. "I never took much to the idea of not telling you about your son. But you know the O'Halleran women. They get that we'll-do-it-my-way-or-else expression on their faces and there's no denying them. Charlie favors you, doesn't he?"

Corey undid the straps of the stroller and tugged Charlie out into his arms. The boy was surprisingly compact, and Corey felt a surge of pride as he thought, *My son's going to be an athlete.* Which was quickly replaced with *My son is so smart* as Charlie giggled and tugged at his ears. *My son is a handsome boy. My son will grow up to be tall— look at those feet, strong and sturdy!—my son will be like me.*

And then pride gave way to a new emotion— love. Corey loved this Charlie, even if he was digging his little fingers into Corey's earlobes with giddy delight.

The only way to be a father to him, Corey thought, was to persuade Robyn to marry. Charlie would not be raised by another man. Charlie would not be raised by a single mom. Charlie would be his son, in every way. And that meant Robyn would be his wife.

In every way.

Corey had never proposed to a woman, and had declined several proposals—each with a great show of regret, as he understood it to be a tremendous emotional exposure for a woman to ask a man to wed. Corey had always assumed that if he decided to ask a woman, she would happily say yes.

Robyn was different.

Robyn was a challenge.

A handful.

Trouble.

She always had been.

He'd marry her. He'd marry her but it wouldn't be against her will. No, he had until Saturday to persuade her. To charm her. To woo her. To make love to her.

He planned his next words carefully, as Robyn stepped up to take Charlie from his arms.

If he didn't have the chance to make love to her, he'd resort to plan B: Aunt Rose.

"We're getting married, Aunt Rose," he said cheerfully. "On Saturday. I understand it's an Irish custom to ask the girl's parents for permission."

Aunt Rose made a face like she was eating a lemon, and he knew he had an ally.

"Bob got it a little backward, didn't he?" she asked.

"Does Robyn have your blessing to marry me?"

Aunt Rose's smile was wider and more sparkling than he could have hoped for.

"Married? Oh, at last, at last!" she cried. "My blessing? Of course, you have it."

"Wonderful," Corey said, shooting Robyn a triumphant smile.

"This calls for a celebration," Rose said.

"No, it's not like that," Robyn said.

She gave him a look that should have made him hang his head, but instead he took Charlie back in his arms. Robyn ran off after her aunt.

"It's not what you think!" Robyn cried.

But Aunt Rose was already halfway up the stairs to the White Lace and Promises shop, saying she had to call the women in her bridge group with the good news.

Over the course of the next hour, the White Lace and Promises store became crowded with an unofficial party for the neighborhood.

Moms came over because their children rushed home with news that Aunt Rose was giving out free cookies to celebrate. Grandparents came because they knew Aunt Rose throwing a party meant laughter, music and a potent orange sherbet punch. Dads came because when they got home from work there were notes in kitchens saying that the family would be back soon—but anybody with a lick of sense would know that stopping in on a party given by Aunt Rose is a several-hour operation.

Bolts of felt served as children's cushions and the long seamstress table became a buffet. Someone put on the CDs of swing and jazz music that Aunt Rose loved. The bell over the door jingled constantly, announcing even more revelers. The bridge group argued mightily over whether Robyn should register for her gifts at Lord & Taylor or Marshall Field's, both Chicago stores of sterling reputation. People took sides on whether Bob would ever recover from being dumped and, if so, which unattached sisters, aunts and cousins had dibs on being introduced to him.

Corey stood behind the cash register with Charlie and took his share of congratulations and even an occasional, confidential "I never thought Bob was man enough for Robyn." Across the store, Robyn was backed up against a rack of organdy ribbon, arms crossed over her chest, repeatedly telling well-wishers that she and Corey weren't in fact getting married.

But one look at Corey, beaming as he held up his son, was enough corroborating evidence for the guests—why else would Aunt Rose lay out such a nice spread? At last Robyn threw up her hands in surrender and accepted a glass of punch.

But when Aunt Rose answered the ringing phone with a cheery "White Lace and Promises," she paled and held a silencing hand up in the air.

Marge, Rose's friend from down the block, flipped off the music.

Conversations abruptly stopped.

Children who had been playing tag froze in their tracks and the shop was as quiet as a funeral parlor.

"It's Bob," Aunt Rose said grimly.

Corey would later conclude that he should have taken the phone out of Aunt Rose's hand and told his romantic rival that Robyn was getting married...and taking the name Harte.

But he was so sure of himself—so sure, in part, because his professional life had never included a no from nurses, patients, staff or younger colleagues. And so sure, in part, because he'd thought that when she'd given up explaining herself to these guests, however sullenly, it had meant there was no more to explain.

He didn't care how he persuaded her to marry, it was the fact that they would that was important.

She would marry the father of her son, and they would be a family.

Simple as that.

He was content to watch her as she listened to Bob on the telephone. He shared a smile with Aunt Rose and confidently jogged Charlie on his hip as Robyn continued nodding and pushing her copper hair behind her ear when it fell onto her face.

He should have noticed that the conversation was lasting a little long for "Sorry, I'm getting married to Corey Harte."

But then she turned away from him, as if he were the intruder, and he started to worry when she continued her long-distance conversation.

She murmured a goodbye, an "I'll see you Saturday" and then hung up. She would not look at Corey, but walked directly across the center aisle of the shop to her aunt's side.

"Did you tell Bob that Corey is back?" Aunt Rose asked.

Robyn ducked her head.

"No. I didn't."

"Did he ever ask his mother?"

"No, he didn't," Robyn said, and Corey let out a long-held breath of relief.

But then she added the fatal words, looking directly at him, with a challenging tilt to her chin.

"Bob's mother has fallen ill and he doesn't want to upset her by talking to her today about our engagement," she said. "But he asked me, anyway—to marry him as soon as he returns home from Ireland on Saturday afternoon. And I said yes."

Chapter Six

Corey lay on the down-filled couch in the second-floor apartment. His head was supported by a chintz pillow covered with a crocheted antimacassar. His knees were propped up, both because if he extended his feet he'd knock over every knick-knack on the end table and because little Charlie needed something to lean his back against while sitting on Corey's stomach. Corey tugged his tie and unbuttoned the top button on his oxford cloth shirt.

Sunlight was diffused through the living room by lace curtains and scattered with glistening dust motes. The scent of roses and talcum powder lingered on the upholstered furniture.

It would have been a very calming atmosphere were it not for the feeling Corey had of having just had the rug snatched out from under him. And indeed, many of the revelers who had slunk out of the White Lace and Promises shop moments after Robyn's announcement, felt exactly the same way.

Saturday she was marrying Bob.

He had failed.

He didn't like Bob, suspected that nothing would change his mind about the man who had won Robyn's hand and heart.

He'd have to make the best of things. Have to watch the only woman he had ever loved marry another man. Have to watch the mother of his only child give herself to someone else. Have to share the experience of fatherhood with a man he was sure he wouldn't like and equally sure he couldn't respect.

He'd have to work out weekends and holidays and who got to sit where at graduations, when all he wanted to do was live like a family. He would have to miss the little things that mattered big-time but couldn't be counted on to happen at the right time on a custody schedule, like Charlie losing his first tooth or learning to ride a bike.

Corey would have done anything to get Robyn to say yes to marriage. Crooked or otherwise, ethical or not, straightforward—well, not if it wouldn't work.

He didn't care—he would have stolen her outright.

Pre-engaged? It made no sense.

But her being engaged was different.

It was just one step, and three days, from being married. He had never stolen another man's woman, never so much as flirted with a woman wearing another man's ring, didn't believe in what some of his less-eloquent male friends called "poaching."

She was off-limits.

But still, this little guy sitting on his stomach, chewing his tie within an inch of choking him, was his child. Charlie belonged to him.

And Robyn belonged to him—try as he might, he couldn't imagine that Robyn rightfully belonged to another man.

Especially a guy who had to ask his mother's permission to get married.

Saturday. Saturday. Saturday.

He had until Saturday to hope that fate would deal him a new hand of cards.

Corey took his son's hand and rubbed it along his jaw.

"Daddy," he said. And then he directed Charlie's hand back to his own stomach. "Charlie. Now, look here, I'm Daddy. You're Charlie. Daddy. Charlie. Daddy. Charlie. Now you try it."

Charlie giggled and poked Corey's chest.

"Cow-ee," he said, quite proud of himself. He put his chubby hand to his own chest. "Chaw-wee. You Cow-ee. Chaw-wee. Cow-ee. You twy."

Corey drew his eyebrows together, which provoked another round of giggles.

"Daddy," he corrected.

"Cow-ee," Charlie insisted.

"He's smart but a mite stubborn," Aunt Rose

said, putting a glass of lemonade on the low table in front of the couch. "And he has trouble with *R*s."

"It doesn't take an *R* to say daddy."

"Dad's a mighty big concept."

"Does he call Bob anything?"

"Just Bob. He doesn't call him Daddy if that's what you're worried about."

"Then he'll learn to call me Daddy," Corey said. "I'll be patient. After all, I've got eighteen years before he gets out of college."

Aunt Rose sat in a well-worn chair that fitted snugly along her hips.

"It must be quite a shock," she said.

"Of course it is."

"A lot of feelings."

"There was a minute of anger."

"She really thought she was doing the right thing not telling you."

"I know. And after I got over being white-hot mad at her, I suddenly felt like I had always wanted to be a dad—even though, if you asked me yesterday I would have said sure I'd like to be a dad, but not for another ten years at least."

"And now?"

"Now I look at him, and I want to be with him all the time," Corey said, poking Charlie's stomach. "Nothing else seems important except..."

"Except what?"

He wasn't a man inclined to share things. In fact,

the work of the past four years had been to rise above emotions. To push past limits imposed by the body—or the heart.

But he had always had a natural, easy affection for Aunt Rose. She was also his ally in this cause.

"I looked at her and I thought I got over her but I didn't. I really didn't. I want her. I wanted us to be together. Like a real family. But now..."

Rose's strong hand reached out to squeeze his.

"Now there's Bobby McNitt," she said. "I thought all his talk of marriage would collapse when he was faced with his formidable ma. But he's done proposed and Robyn's said yes. And if she puts her mind to do something, there's nothing on heaven or earth that'll stop her. Including you. And are you really the kind of man who would try to break up a marriage?"

"Engagement," Corey corrected.

"Are you?"

"No. It would be wrong of me."

"Aunt Rose, I thought you liked Bob," Robyn said. She came into the living room with a towel draped across her neck. She had showered and changed into a pair of worn-at-the-knees jeans and a white, pocket T-shirt. Her hair fell around her shoulders in damp, dark curls. Her face was scrubbed to a shine. He liked her this way.

His expression must have given him away, because she gave him a stern look.

Charlie, seeing his mother, slid off Corey's

stomach and went to sit on Robyn's lap. She picked him up and kissed him on both candy-stained cheeks.

"What's not to like about Bob?" Rose mused, sitting back in her chair and picking up some tatting. "He did my taxes last year and saved me three hundred dollars. And he came to my bridge group and explained the difference between whole-term life insurance and graduated annuities."

"What is the difference?" Corey asked.

Rose shrugged.

"She was caught napping during the talk," Robyn said, rocking back and forth with Charlie's head on her shoulder. The tyke twisted one of her curls around his hand.

"I wasn't napping," Rose said with great dignity. "I was resting my eyes so that my brain could stay focused."

"Bob sounds like a winner," Corey said. "Devoted to his mother, possessed of a rare and sparkling conversational style...."

"Don't do it, Corey," Robyn said firmly.

"What am I doing?"

"You know what you're doing. You're trying to diminish Bob in my eyes."

"Why would I do a thing like that? Is it perhaps because you should marry me?"

She kissed Charlie's forehead. "Aunt Rose, I think it's dinnertime."

Her aunt hoisted herself to her feet.

"Come along, Charlie," she said. "They never let us listen to the good stuff."

Looking back once to his mom for encouragement, Charlie took Aunt Rose's hand. After the door to the kitchen closed behind them, Robyn leaned forward so that her face was mere inches from Corey's.

"I am marrying a very nice man," she said. "You are not to make fun of him. Or make snide or teasing remarks. Especially not in front of Charlie. Or Aunt Rose. You talk about eighteen years being rough, Corey. It will be if you keep this up."

He liked her being this close. Even if she was mad. Her breasts nearly, but not quite, grazed his arm. They were fuller, more rounded than he remembered. Memories of that sweet lovemaking flooded through him. He propped his knee up so that the evidence of his thoughts wouldn't be apparent.

How sweet it was to make love to her! And then he thought of Bob. The one-syllable name in his head was like getting whacked on the side of the head with a blast of cold water.

"I'm not making fun of him," he said, then he amended his declaration when her eyes flared like burning emeralds, "All right, I am. But I can't see you marrying this guy. He's all wrong for you."

"Oh, really?"

"Yes, really."

"And you're not saying this because you want me to marry you?"

"Not just that. I'm also saying this because he's just not right for you. I'm looking out for your best interests, Robyn."

"You don't know the first thing about him."

"I know the first thing about you," Corey said, trapping her arms on either side of him. "I made love to you. If you don't want to believe it, there's proof in the kitchen. And I know Bob can't give you the passion you need, the passion you once had, the passion you crave and will always crave."

Robyn squirmed, but he held firm to her.

"Corey, let me go."

"Not before you kiss me. Really kiss me."

"I won't. It's wrong. It's cheating. I'm engaged to be married. I'm going to be Mrs. Bob McNitt in just three days."

"If we're going to coparent, we need to be courteous and cooperative with each other. Friendly, too."

"Friendly doesn't include kisses," she replied, tugging hard but gaining no purchase. In fact, losing several vital inches so that her breasts were now pressed against his chest and her lips were mere centimeters from infidelity. "Courteous and cooperative doesn't mean grabbing me like this."

"A courteous and cooperative peck on the lips. Just one," Corey insisted. "If you're right and I'm wrong, if there isn't anything left between us, fine.

If there isn't that deep well of passion in you, then I'll withdraw my objection to your marriage. If you can kiss me just once and get up and walk away, I'll welcome that man back to America with a hearty handshake.''

''I won't be able to get up if you've got your arms around me like this,'' she said through gritted teeth.

He let her go, nearly sending her tumbling to the floor. But she recovered and perched daintily on the inch of upholstery that was left over after he placed his arms chastely across his chest.

''If you can kiss me without the slightest…urgings, I promise I'll never bring this up again. We'll coparent the modern way. I'll offer my congratulations to Bob on his fine choice of a bride, and I'll do my best to be a friend to him.''

Robyn narrowed her eyes.

''No tricks?''

He closed his eyes.

''No tricks. I'm just going to lie here and wait for you to kiss me.''

''I've done a lot of growing up in the past four years,'' Robyn warned. ''I've had to learn to be responsible for my actions, to take care of others, to make hard choices.''

''No doubt that's true.''

''You don't bring out the best in me. When we made love, I was irresponsible, I wasn't thinking straight, I was moved by forces beyond my control.

Now I'm hardworking, responsible, steady, secure…''

"Snore."

"And I don't want to be out of control again."

"I understand perfectly," Corey said, squeezing
his eyes hard. He could smell her, vanilla and talc
and Ivory soap. It nearly drove him crazy. But he
willed his arms to not reach for her, tucking his
fingers under his forearms. "Just kiss me once.
Friendly-like. Then I'll never bring this marriage
stuff up again."

"I really don't think I should," she said. "It's
unfair to Bob."

He opened his eyes. She looked tormented. Her
head hung low, her hair falling in front of her face.
He nearly felt sorry for her.

But then he remembered that he was a father
now.

No mercy.

"Robyn, I want that kiss."

She jerked her head up. Her cheeks were hot
pink, and she licked her lips and he thought to
himself, *I've got her now.*

*I've got my bride, my son and Judge Campbell
has penciled me in for Saturday.*

He wondered what the time difference was between Chicago and Ireland and if it would be too
much to ask her to break up with Bob right away
or should he advise letting Bob know he was being
dumped in person—on Saturday.

It was probably kinder to tell Bob he wasn't having a wedding *before* he brought up the subject of marriage to his mother.

"I don't think this is a good idea," she repeated.

It was a terrible one, he thought triumphantly.

Terrible for her, terrible for Bob.

Wonderful for him. There was something magical between them, something like destiny, and if he felt its reawakening, surely a kiss would do the same for her.

Her resistance was weakening. He would be gentle, even refuse to make love to her right now. Wait. Better strategy to get her to the altar. That was the most important thing.

"Robyn, when Bob comes back to Chicago and meets me, you'll want to have not the slightest doubt about your feelings. You wouldn't want him to be afraid that I'd steal his wife."

"I don't know..."

"And you wouldn't want to have those doubts lurking inside of you—ready to blow your marriage to Bob right out of the water."

"Maybe you're right."

"I know I'm right." He closed his eyes again. "Friendly peck."

"All right, friendly peck."

She leaned over and touched her lips against his. He tensed his muscles, didn't move, although his instinct was to take her into his embrace. He opened his lips, waiting for her sweetness.

She would feel it. The magic. The passion. The power.

She would know she was meant to be his, as surely as she'd known it the first time they made love.

He opened his mouth, groaning with pleasure mixed with triumph, his fingers agitating to pull her closer. Not yet, he warned himself. Let her take the lead or she'll bolt. He remained totally still, waiting for her tongue to enter his open, willing mouth.

And suddenly he felt...nothing.

He opened his eyes, saw a glimpse of denim and bare feet as the kitchen door swung shut, and then he realized the awful truth.

He was a failure.

He was a broken man.

He had tried to seduce—and failed.

He had tried using Aunt Rose as an ally—and failed.

But that wasn't the worst of it.

The worst of it was that she really, truly, in her heart, didn't want him anymore.

Chapter Seven

He walked into the kitchen several minutes later, after having dunked his head in the bathroom sink filled with cold water. He sat at the table next to Charlie's booster seat and solemnly regarded his son.

Charlie giggled.

"Cow-ee," he said, pointing.

Like a broken man, Corey sighed heavily. He didn't have the energy to say "Daddy."

"Chaw-ee," Charlie said.

Charlie picked up a piece of cereal that was part of the pile put on his plate every evening to keep him satisfied while his mom and aunt put the finishing touches on dinner.

"Cow-ee?" he asked, holding out the cereal to Corey.

Corey took it, mustered a half-hearted smile, and put the piece of cereal on his tongue. It tasted like cardboard. And he had always liked Cheerios.

Aunt Rose put a platter of roast beef and mashed potatoes in the middle of the table. Corey could still remember meals he'd had in this apartment when he was visiting from college—hearty meals that gave not an inch to the culinary trends of nouvelle cuisine and post-nouvelle cuisine and post-post-nouvelle cuisine. Real-people food. The roast beef and potatoes and green beans in a bowl that Robyn put on the table should have made him salivate. Besides, he hadn't eaten since a quick breakfast at the hospital cafeteria after surgery and before morning rounds.

But he had no appetite.

From her seat at the head of the table, Aunt Rose regarded him thoughtfully.

"We should say grace," she said.

She took Charlie's and Robyn's hand and gestured for Corey to do the same from his end of the table. When Robyn tentatively gave Corey her hand, he was so distracted by Charlie's pudgy fingers enmeshed in his left hand that he barely registered the trembling of the slim fingers he held in his right.

If he had noticed, his mood might have changed dramatically.

Instead, he thought of Charlie and how the little hand in his would grow. Eighteen years and he'd be a man. And Corey would have done his job as a father—except his job would be shared with another man and would be regulated by a schedule.

"We thank Thee, Heavenly Father, for returning Corey to our home," Aunt Rose began. "We have kept him in our hearts for four years and we ask for Your guidance to reignite the love we—"

Robyn cleared her throat.

"All right, all right," Aunt Rose said. "And for all the gifts Thy blessings bring. Amen."

After the amen, Corey slipped the napkin out from the side of Charlie's plate and put it on his lap. Robyn cut a piece of meat into tiny pieces, and Charlie dug in heartily. Corey glumly pushed his vegetables around his plate.

He knew he should be grateful that Charlie was healthy, that Charlie was a fine boy, that at least Robyn wasn't putting up a fight about him seeing Charlie. That should be enough of a blessing, enough of a wonder for him to say his own special grace.

"I haven't had any experience with broken families," he said.

"We call it blended," Robyn said gently. "It sounds better, don't you think?"

"I suppose," Corey said. "Anyhow, I haven't had any experience at it—or even at being a father. But I'll do my best. Starting with money. I'll pay for everything. I don't ever want him to need anything he doesn't have, and I don't want you to feel your only recourse is to do without or to go to court. So just give me all the bills. The trust fund won't even need to be touched."

"That's very generous," Robyn said evenly. "But I have a job."

"You don't have to work anymore. You can stay home with Charlie."

"I do now—at least, a lot of the time. I just go out when I'm meeting clients. I'm very happy working. I would like more time with Charlie, but every working mother feels that way. Don't try to change me."

"No, no, I'm not," he said quickly. "I just want you to know that you have the financial security to stay at home with Charlie. Now, have you and Bob picked out a place to live after you marry?"

Aunt Rose and Robyn exchanged a meaning-laden glance.

"Bob was going to move in here," Robyn said. "He puts a lot of his salary as an accountant away because he wants to retire early."

"You can't stay here. This apartment's way too small," Corey said, correcting himself quickly as he saw her flash of indignation. "I just think we should buy a large house that can be subdivided into two sections. One for you and Bob and the other for me. And Aunt Rose can be on my side to make it even. Us being together would make Charlie's life a lot easier."

He caught Robyn's heavy sigh, but he plowed ahead.

"I'd like to give you and Bob a gift of a honeymoon. My wedding present. Anywhere in the world you want to go. Of course I hope you'll leave Charlie with Aunt Rose and me.''

Robyn looked down at her plate.

''That's very generous of you.''

''And I want you to know that even though I have a lot of love for you, I will keep the inappropriate feelings under wraps—I won't ever put your husband on the spot. Because, Robyn, I love you in a lot of different ways. Like a little sister, like a friend, like—''

She glanced at him sharply.

''But I won't ever mention it again.''

She nodded.

''Let me be his daddy,'' Corey pleaded. ''Don't shut me out again. I appreciate what you did when you didn't tell me about Charlie—you would have been absolutely right if you thought I wouldn't finish my residency if I knew you were carrying my child. But don't shut me out any longer.''

Several long moments passed, the silence punctuated only by the vroom-vrooming of Charlie making his green beans tunnel through his mashed potatoes.

''Don't look like nobody's eating my cooking,'' Aunt Rose observed.

Robyn's eyes sparkled with tears.

''All right, I'm sorry. Would you like to stay and help with giving Charlie his bath?''

AFTER DINNER Aunt Rose announced she was going to her bedroom.

Corey left a voice mail message for the chairwoman of the evening's Arthritis Association Gala telling her that he had unexpectedly found himself unable to attend. He checked in for messages at his clinic and was relieved when told that none of his patients needed his attention—but he left Aunt Rose's phone number in case he was needed later in the evening.

Then he called Ashford Pinksmith III.

"Find it?" he asked grimly.

"Yeah, it was in my dresser. Do you still want me to pick it up?"

"I guess not. Robyn's engaged to another man."

Ashford whistled.

"That's rough, buddy. But you'll work it out. I don't think you're meant for marriage anyhow."

"What makes you say that?"

"I've never seen you settle down with a woman for long."

"I've never had a son before."

"You got a point there," Ashford said. "Now what do I do with the receipt?"

"Keep it. I'll pick it up from you tomorrow and take it back to Tiffany's."

"Think they've still got the ring? Four years is a mighty long time."

"It doesn't matter much, if she's marrying another guy."

"You know, Corey, you're not the depressed type but you're sounding terribly low."

"Wouldn't you be?"

"Sure. But I know exactly what I'd do."

"What?"

"I'd come to you, explain my problem and have you solve it."

After saying goodbye, he followed Robyn's directions through the whole ritual of getting Charlie ready for bed.

First choosing five, six, Mommy-one-more? toys for the bath.

Then tussling with the T-shirt over Charlie's head, the shorts, the Pull-Ups underwear, the socks.

Third, after Charlie gave a shout at the freedom of nakedness, chasing the little boy around the apartment.

Finally came the calibration of the water temperature—an exacting science requiring Charlie to put his toe in and scream "Too hot!" even when the water was lukewarm.

And Corey did all these things without once looking down Robyn's neckline as she leaned over him to turn on the water, without once noticing the feel of her hair caressing his face as she put in the bubbles, without lingering in his gaze as she crawled under the couch to pull Charlie out.

"Does Bob help with this?" Corey called as he sat by the bathtub watching Charlie.

"I only let Bob meet him recently," Robyn said, coming back into the bathroom with a set of Power

Rangers pajamas. "We've taken Charlie to the movies and to a restaurant. And Bob sometimes takes him to the park on Saturdays. I didn't want to introduce Charlie to a man unless it was serious."

"That's wise. How does Bob feel about Charlie?"

"Loves him very much. But he's definitely looking forward to having other children."

"Other children?" The idea of Robyn having a baby by another man hadn't occurred to Corey, but he found it instantly troubling. Where would Charlie's place be in such a family? And why should Bob want his own children? Wasn't Charlie enough for him?

"That's what married people do—they have children," Robyn reminded him. "Now, could you pick him up out of the bathtub?"

"No, Mommy! Not done."

"Charlie, we go through this every night," Robyn said. "Bathtime's over."

"No-o-o-!"

"I'll watch him," Corey volunteered. "Just a few extra minutes."

Robyn gave in because she could use the extra time. She washed the dishes, checked her voice mail for messages from clients, then realized it was ten o'clock.

"It's late," she said, coming back into the bathroom. Corey sat by the tub, raising a plastic boat against Charlie. "Bedtime."

"Mommy!"

"It's really bedtime," she said.

Charlie knew when he had pushed too far and he willingly put his arms up so Corey could pull him out of the bathtub. Robyn helped him with his pajamas and directed his efforts at brushing his teeth.

"Usually we read a story, but I'm just too tired," she said.

"I'll do it," Corey said. "You go and do what you have to do."

She looked at him.

"I'm serious," he said. "I've got a lot of time to make up for. Let's start me off tonight. I'll read him a story."

"Then afterward put him to bed?"

"Where does he sleep?"

"In the alcove by my bedroom."

"I'll hold off on telling him about how he could have a big bedroom if we all got a big house."

"Good. Because I'm too tired to listen."

She went to bed, closing the door firmly behind her. And then reconsidering, opening it just a crack.

"I don't want company," she said. "This door stays closed."

"I won't try anything ever again," Corey said

wearily. "You're a married woman. Or practically one, anyway."

Corey located the alcove bed, but it was too small for him to stretch out. He took Charlie to the living room and they lay together on the couch while he read a Seuss book. By the last page Charlie was asleep, and Corey didn't want to move him.

He let his eyes drift shut, the rhythmic breathing of his newfound son acting as a lullaby. It had been a long day—starting off with a 4:00 a.m. emergency surgery. And a tumultuous one—he had woken up as an unencumbered bachelor and ended the day a father on the brink of an oddly modern, sure-to-be-uncomfortable family.

But he had his son, and he wasn't ever letting go.

Even as it broke his heart to think of how things had turned out.

He was jolted out of his rest by the phone ringing. He instantly remembered he had left this number with his service. He clamped a hand down on the phone and picked up, easing Charlie out of the way as he put the receiver to his ear.

"Dr. Harte."

The whistling and clicking of a long-distance connection, and not a very good one at that, followed.

"Dr. Harte?" A tentative male voice replied. "I must have the wrong number. I was calling for Miss Robyn O'Halleran."

"Robyn? Oh, she's asleep."

"And who did you say you are?"

"Dr. Harte."

"Are you the old man?"

Corey woke up. Truly woke up.

He wondered what she had said about him. Had she even mentioned him or acknowledged him as Charlie's father? Had she said she loved him once?

"Yeah, I am," he lied. "The old man. That's me—very old. I just came by for a visit. A visit with Aunt Rose. Old times' sake, nostalgia and whatnot."

"I'll talk to Aunt Rose, then."

"Sorry, she's...uh..." He glanced down the hall to Aunt Rose's closed bedroom door. "She's asleep, too. Who are you?"

But he already knew the answer.

He wasn't the slightest bit surprised when the caller announced that he was Bob McNitt.

Calling long-distance from Ireland.

Chapter Eight

When Robyn's alarm went off at seven o'clock, she showered and dressed, choosing a pale peach linen suit that she ordinarily kept for her most important meetings. She took extra care with her makeup and was pleased that not a single strand of her rich russet-colored hair was acting disobedient.

She looked every inch the professional, in-control woman, and that was exactly what she needed today.

"When I was a little girl, I had a crush on a man," she told herself in the bathroom mirror and she slipped on tiny pearl post earrings. "I had a crush, acted foolishly for just one night and ended up with the greatest blessing of my life. But I learned a lot from the experience. About stupid choices and smart decisions. About men in shock. And about self-discipline."

And she had that last in spades this morning.

After all, she had passed the ultimate test of her mettle.

She had kissed Corey Harte and escaped—well, at least resisted temptation—unscathed. It was the equivalent of leaving a last butter-pecan, chocolate-chip cookie in the package—multiplied a zillion times over.

"I'm a businesswoman, a professional, a mother, an adult. I work hard. I make deadlines. I keep my customers satisfied," she recounted to herself as she put on her slim gold watch. "My business makes all its loan payments on time. I am resourceful, focused and disciplined, and I never give in to impulse."

She picked up the framed picture of Bob she kept on her nightstand. He wore a starched white shirt, a yellow silk tie, and his pale hair was clipped as short as an astronaut's. His glasses had dark plastic frames, but even so, you could look in his eyes and see that he was a good man. Such a good, decent man. He brought out the best in her.

All the things she had become in the past four years were embodied in her relationship with him.

"We're not waiting any longer to marry," she said, feeling a break in her confidence. "Marry me, Bob. If you love me like you say you do, you'd better marry me. And quick. Saturday wouldn't be too soon."

Remembering that she had a fitting with a client and a walk-through of a fabric warehouse on her agenda, she pulled a pair of low-heeled pumps from her closet. The aroma of coffee and Charlie's babbling lured her to the kitchen.

"Whoo-ee, Mommy, you look good," Corey said, sitting next to Charlie's booster seat. "Doesn't she?"

Charlie nodded vigorously.

Robyn kissed Charlie good-morning on his cheek. He grabbed for, and got, another kiss.

Corey's suit was wrinkled, his shirt had a stain on it that must be Charlie's drool. His tie was askew, and his jaw sported a day's worth of stubble.

But he still was more handsome than the rest of the male population!

"Except Bob, of course," Robyn murmured, feeling like a traitor.

"Don't I get one of those kisses?"

He had his hands clasped behind his head, looking as if he didn't have a care in the world. Looking a little smug, in fact.

Quite a change from the previous evening when Robyn had nearly given him a hug good-night, just because he looked so depressed, so low, so brought down.

Now he looked relaxed, vibrant and a little like he had a secret he wasn't going to share.

But I'm the one with the secret, she thought indignantly.

She wagged a finger at him. "No kiss for you.

I thought we agreed we're not going to spend the next eighteen years teasing and flirting and making double entendres.''

"There's nothing double about it. I want a good-morning kiss.''

"I'm engaged.''

"So what? We're coparents. Just a kiss—you can confine it to the cheek if it makes you feel better,'' he said, giving her a wide-eyed, puppy-dog stare. "You want Charlie to grow up with us as good role models for cooperative parenting, don't you?''

She glanced at Charlie who was watching the back-and-forth as solemnly and attentively as a fan at Wimbledon.

"Fine,'' she said.

She leaned over the table and kissed the air next to Corey's face. He reached to grab her for more, but she stepped back quickly.

"That'll do,'' she snapped. "Why are you here so early?''

"Because I never left. I fell asleep on the couch.''

Robyn got a cup of coffee and handed the salt shaker to Aunt Rose and she finished scrambling eggs.

"It's not a good idea for you to sleep over. Don't do it again.''

"You're right. This apartment is too crowded for a sleepover. That's why I thought that after the caterer calls me back I should take all of us over to my house. I think we can divide it quite nicely so that all of us can live together.''

"All of us?"

"Bob will love the arrangement," Corey said, thanking Aunt Rose for the heaping plate of eggs, bacon, toast and orange slices she put before him. "I won't charge you two lovebirds rent. He can save even more for his retirement."

"We're not moving."

"Let's wait till after the caterer calls. We'll see the place, and then if you think Bob will like it, we'll move in. Actually, I know Bob will like it. It's free."

"I'm all for seeing it," Aunt Rose said, putting a small plate of dry toast at Robyn's place. "Corey says I'd have my own suite. With a Jacuzzi in the bathroom and a sitting room for entertaining my friends."

"Aunt Rose!"

"And he's ordered an orthopedic bed for me. I haven't had a good night's sleep on my own bed in ten years. It'll be quite a relief if a new bed works."

Robyn sank to her seat.

"We're not moving," she insisted. "And what's a caterer got to do with it?"

"I'm thinking a light menu," Corey said, forking up a healthy chunk of eggs. "A little salad, dainty watercress sandwiches or maybe a quiche. I'll just bet Bob likes quiche.''

"As a matter of fact, he does. But what are you catering?''

"A wedding. Your wedding.''

"I'm not marrying you.''

"You're marrying somebody. You have until Saturday to decide who the groom is. If you don't choose me, I'm throwing you and Bob a wedding. Saturday. One-ish. Just like the judge said. I hope you'll let me walk you down the aisle if I lose you,'' he added with a mischievous grin. "And a Saturday wedding would settle this family situation once and for all, wouldn't it?''

She felt ill.

She pushed her plate away.

He smiled wickedly.

"I told Corey that Bob had been upset when he found out how much it costs to throw a decent wedding,'' Aunt Rose said, sitting down at the head of the table. "And that Bob thought it would be better to just drive down to the county clerk's office. I suspect that's what you're thinking of doing when he comes back.''

Robyn wagged her finger at her aunt. "You're aiding and abetting the enemy,'' she warned.

"Guilty as charged,'' her aunt replied.

"That Bob,'' Corey said, smacking his lips. "Such a romantic. But wait a minute! You can't get married on Saturday to Bob. You don't have a license, and Illinois has that twenty-four-hour waiting period.''

"I got the license," Robyn said quietly.

Corey put his toast down on his plate.

Aunt Rose made the sign of the cross and shook her head.

"Yeah, but who paid for it?" Corey asked.

"Excuse me?"

"Who paid for it?"

"I did, but Bob's going to pay me back. It's just I was the one who went to the clerk's office to pick up the forms, and he had already left for Ireland so..."

"Bob's gonna stiff you on the cost of the license," Corey warned triumphantly. "What do you think, Aunt Rose?"

"It's a risk."

"I won't stand for this!" Robyn exclaimed. She stood up, and Charlie gave her an anguished look. She softened her next words. "Corey Harte, I want to talk to you. Right now. In my bedroom."

Corey winked at Charlie and gave him a thumb's-up. Charlie used both his hands to squeeze one into a fist and then laboriously popped out his thumb.

Robyn turned on her heels and led Corey into the bedroom.

"You seem to have forgotten what we worked out last night," she said, shutting the door behind him. "You at least have enough of a sense of honor to recognize that I'm engaged. I thought we agreed that meant no touching, no flirting, no teasing, no…''

"I've decided to act unethically."

Of all the answers he could have given, this one shocked Robyn the most. The Corey she had known had always carefully considered the consequences of his actions, had always played by a fair set of rules, even when it wasn't to his own advantage, had always had a well-defined set of ethics.

"Unethically?"

"I'm going after you. Unethical, yes. Necessary, absolutely."

"Then what's all this talk about coparenting?"

"Coparenting is only plan B," he said, advancing on her. She backed against the dresser, and when he continued his approach, her fall-back position was the wall. He stepped so there were scant inches between them. His knee grazed the space between her legs. "Plan A is seduction. Operation Steal Bob's Fiancée. Mission Objective—marriage to the mother of my child. I have two days. Two days where I will devote myself to the noble cause of bringing my son's parents together. Nobly and unethically."

With a firm hand on each side of her waist, he pulled her up to him for a kiss, but she shoved him back with an open palm on his face.

"What happens when I get married on Saturday?"

He clamped his hand on her wrist and brought her hand down behind her back.

"If you choose me on Saturday, life is going to be pretty dandy. If you choose Bob, well, I'll throw you a wedding and try to be a good sport. We can live together as one big happy family."

He dropped his head as if to take a kiss, the same kiss she had refused to give him willingly. Bending at her knees, she slid down the wall so that her head was even with the knot of his tie. Her eyes strained upward to meet his gaze without giving him the advantage of a clear path to her parted lips.

"I'm not going to use force," he said, planting one hand on the wall next to her right shoulder and the other hand next to her left. "And you'll notice I'm not even touching you."

"But you're trying to seduce me."

"Sure am. But I'll do it fair and square. Sort of. I have an advantage because I'm a man and Bob's a mouse."

"Corey…"

"You're going to want me. You're going to ask me to make love to you. And you're just the kind of woman who, after we make love, will want to marry me."

She would have liked to slap that knowing, arrogant look right off his face. Instead she smiled.

A little wistful around the edges, full of promise and the kind of adoration that could make a man feel ten feet tall. Robyn had never tried such a smile on a man, but she was twenty-three years old and now was just as good a time to learn as any.

"All right," she said a little breathlessly, putting her index finger to his chest. "I'm going to ask right now."

He groaned. His hips pressed ever so lightly against her skirt. His knee dug farther into the space between her legs.

"Ask me, Robyn," he said. His voice was ragged and his lips nearly, but not quite, touched her forehead. "Ask me now."

He dropped his head to her collarbone, nuzzling her delicate flesh.

"Please…"

"Yes, I'll make love to you," Corey promised. "It'll be so good between us."

"I'm asking you now, Corey. Please."

"Yes, you ask, baby, and I'll say yes."

"Please get off me!"

She pushed hard, hard enough that he ended up sprawled on the floor. The brisk click of her heels down the hardwood floor was his only consolation. He heard in that step a certain O'Halleran outrage.

He shrugged. He had two days.

He got up and looked around the femininely decorated room. A quilt-covered bed. A desk with a bulletin board on which were pinned half a dozen scribblings that he knew must be Charlie's, as well as a drawing by Aunt Rose of a gown with several cloth samples pinned to it. A nightstand with a lamp, a stack of paperback books, a vase of early budding irises and a framed picture.

He picked up the picture, reaching into his shirt pocket for a marker.

He carefully drew a mustache. And then, not completely satisfied, drew two horns on either side of Bob's head.

He threw in a goatee for good measure.

He regarded his work thoughtfully and then felt his conscience kick in.

"Got to feel sorry for the guy," he said, grabbing a tissue and wiping away all trace of his vandalism.

Chapter Nine

Preston True, head chef and president of the catering firm Entre Vous, squirmed at his teak desk. He took a sip of sparkling water from a blue-green venetian glass. He draped one hand in the air, searching for that perfect dramatic gesture or word that would communicate his delight at being chosen to do Corey Harte's wedding.

Like every Chicagoan, he read the society pages. He knew the zillionaire doctor was no more and no less than the most eligible bachelor to be found in a hundred square miles. Corey Harte was tying the knot, and Preston True would be providing the menu.

Now he didn't feel so bad about missing out on the John F. Kennedy, Jr., wedding.

Sure, Saturday was short notice. But celebrity weddings always were spur-of-the-moment. And shrouded in secrecy, although the pair had made no mention of the type of nondisclosure agreements that Preston had heard Hollywood caterers had to make. If they forgot to make him sign, he'd be on the phone with his contact at the *Tribune* as soon as they left.

"I'm thinking..." He brought his hand out to the center of the triangle created by himself and his two new clients seated across from him. Odd how she glared at Corey, but marital bliss was not Preston's concern. "I'm thinking of opening the meal with salmon on toast points with a cracked peppercorn mustard and caramelized onion glaze." He waited for a response. Applause would not be out of the question.

Corey shrugged. "Sure," he said. "What do you think, honey?"

"Bob's allergic to fish," Robyn said firmly. "And while we're discussing the menu, he's also allergic to berries."

Preston looked at Corey and then at Robyn. "And Bob is...someone I should know?"

"My fiancé," Robyn said.

Preston felt his silk shirt droop around his shoulders. Did this mean he wasn't doing Corey Harte's wedding?

"She's marrying me," Corey said. "We have a child together. It's important for us to be together as a family. She's just a little confused."

"You have a child?" Preston asked, thinking that he hadn't heard this tidbit before.

"He's three years old," Corey said. "Just found

out about him yesterday and now I'm going to marry his mom.''

"I'm not marrying you," Robyn said. "I'm marrying Bob. If you plan a wedding, that's your business. But I'll be marrying Bob.''

Preston made a little diagram in his head.

"Refresh my memory. Who is Bob again?"

"My fiancé. He's not here.''

"Obviously," Preston said, waving a hand to indicate that his modern loft office didn't have any hiding places.

"Bob is away. He'll get here on Saturday," Robyn explained. "He's in Ireland. He can't return until the day of the wedding.''

Preston had a sudden insight. Bob. Ireland. Unannounced wedding—Corey Harte's wedding announcement would have ranked a Sunday front page of the Lifestyle section at least and Preston hadn't seen it. Sudden wedding, without even a professional wedding planner. Bride who looked like she might well be a model or an actress. Hmm. Very interesting strategy. Sending Corey Harte to plan out the wedding and act as if he were going to marry her. At the last minute Bob would appear.

Bob must be really famous.

Preston searched his nearly encyclopedic knowledge of supermarket tabloids and concluded that Bob was the lead singer of a superstar band Bumpus that was, this very evening, playing in a stadium in Dublin. Preston was sure he had seen the concert advertised on HBO. The concert would be aired all over the world.

The child was a ruse. Or was he?

Preston was quite pleased.

"Bob," he said, careful to appear quite used to this sort of situation. "Let's talk food. Regardless of who you marry, this is an early-afternoon wedding, and maybe we would like to have a more 'breakfasty-brunch' feel to it. *Non?*"

"That sounds good," Robyn said.

"What does your fiancé, Bob, like to eat for brunch?"

"I don't know."

"In the morning," he prompted. "Brunch is a morning repast. Light and airy. Frothy and fun. What does he likes to eat when he arises? Maybe we could do scrambled eggs with truffles and Portobello mushrooms?"

"We've never had brunch."

"What does Bob usually eat for breakfast?" Corey asked bluntly.

"I said I don't know."

"Pop-Tarts or cereal?"

"We've never had brunch—or breakfast—together."

"I'm not serving cereal, that's for sure." Preston sniffed haughtily. They might be clients, and celebrity ones at that, but a caterer had to be firm. But that grin on Corey's face—it was quite disturbing. Suddenly appearing out of nowhere—as wide as the gridlock on Lake Shore Drive on a Friday afternoon before a holiday weekend.

"Why are you so interested in what Bob eats for breakfast?" Robyn asked Corey, noticing his smile at the same time Preston did. "This isn't just about the wedding. You want to know what he eats. Why should it matter to you?"

"You've never slept over at Bob's house," Corey announced. "And he's never slept over at yours. You haven't slept in the same bed. Ever, I'd bet."

"No, we haven't," Robyn said. "But I don't think that is going to make a difference on the wedding menu. Is it?"

Preston was taken aback by her intense stare. She was really quite beautiful, especially when she was angry. So vital, so full of *joie de vivre*...

"No, I guess you don't have to sleep with a man to plan a brunch menu around him," he allowed.

"Yes, you do," Corey said, that grin only getting bigger. "Robyn, you've never made love to Bob."

Robyn glanced at Preston, but he really couldn't care about whether she had made love to Bob or Corey or both or neither. The chef carefully rubbed the bridge of his nose in a circular motion that was meant to eliminate annoying character lines. Wrinkles, his doctor had called them—and they were coming fast and furious now.

"And so what if I haven't?" she asked.

"That means I've got better-than-even odds that you'll marry me," Corey mused.

"I've heard enough," Robyn said smartly, shoving her chair back from the desk. "Whether I make love to my fiancé or not is none of your business."

"Hold on," Corey said. "I'm going with you. And who you sleep with is my business if you're the mother of my son."

"Wait!" Preston called, one index finger pressed firmly on the bridge of his nose. "Are we doing the wedding or not?"

"Yes," Corey said. "I'm marrying her."

"And what do you want me to feed your guests?"

"I personally like burgers and fries," Corey said. "Real-people food. If she marries Bob, I won't have an appetite."

As the door slammed behind his two newest clients, Preston carefully wrote out *pommes frittes et le hamburger* on his menu pad. On the other form for the bakery, he wrote that the names Robyn and Bob and Corey should be joined on the cake. He'd take a pastry knife to one of the names before the ceremony.

After the ceremony, just to be sure.

He finished the Entre Vous order form with a flourished signature.

And then, only then, did Preston True pick up the phone.

"I THINK it's none of your business, but I'll tell you anyhow, since you seem so interested," Robyn said, crossing her arms over her chest. "I've never made love to him. Satisfied?"

They stood on the steps of the Houston Street warehouse. The sidewalk was empty, the sunlight bounced happily off the roofs of the cars parked in every available spot, and from a distance, a jack-hammer roared.

"Is your curiosity satisfied?" she demanded again.

"Let me just get the facts straight," Corey said, guiding her toward the cab stand by the lightest touch at her elbow. "You've been going out with this guy for how long?"

"Two years."

"And you've never once…?"

"No."

"And why not?"

Robyn stopped short. "Because sex is not the most important thing in a relationship!" she said hotly. Out of the corner of her eye, she noticed a woman leaning out of a second-story window, eyes wide. She dropped her voice. "Bob and I have a relationship based on love and mutual respect, and he knows, we both know, that I made a mistake when I let animal instinct take over. Once."

"Is that what you call Charlie—a mistake?"

"No, of course not. He's the most wonderful boy in the world."

"Then it's Bob who thinks he is a mistake."

She shook a finger at his face. "Don't try to make Bob a villain. He merely thinks, as do I, that I made a mistake letting passion take the place of a committed relationship. And he respects me too much to allow us to make the same mistake. The same mistake I made with you."

"I respected you. And I have mutual interests and ambitions."

"You didn't respect me!" she countered with a vehemence that surprised them both. "You lusted."

"That, too."

"You used me only to satisfy your physical needs."

"I could make love to you a thousand times and I wouldn't be satisfied," Corey said. "I'd still want more. I wanted more that night."

He took one step forward, she took two steps back.

"I wanted more when you wouldn't return my phone calls," he said.

Two steps forward, three steps back.

"I wanted more when the florist said you wouldn't take delivery of my flowers," he said.

Three steps forward, four steps back.

"I wanted more every time I called and Aunt Rose told me you wouldn't talk to me. I wanted more from you. I want more from you now."

He backed her up against a newspaper box.

"I couldn't give you everything that night—a wedding, a ring, a life," Corey said. "But if I could have, I would have."

"It was just physical for you," she insisted, wiggling out of his way. But the *Tribune* newspaper box was next to the *Sun-Times* box and the *Chicago Defender* next to that. He had her. She looked over her shoulder at the intersection. The crossing guard for the school across the street was eating a donut with his attention on a newspaper.

"No, it wasn't just physical," Corey said. "It was magic. It was destiny. It was a lot of things. A lot of things that I could live to be a hundred and a helluva lot wiser, and making love to you would still be a heavenly mystery."

She waved at the crossing guard, but couldn't catch his eye.

"And one other thing, Robyn, I didn't just satisfy myself. It was good for you, too."

She closed her eyes.

"You wanted more, too." he added.

She remembered the wanting. But she vividly remembered the humiliation of wanting and knowing there couldn't be any more.

Why couldn't it be like it was with Bob? Safe and secure and somehow like wearing a pair of flannel pajamas on a cold winter's night.

Instead, she was standing on Huron Street with a drop-dead handsome man with a heavy-lidded gaze that let her know he knew all her body's secrets and wasn't going to do the gentlemanly thing and forget about them.

If the look in his eyes didn't make it clear that he wanted to make love and she would like it, he was happy to tell her. In English. Out loud.

And there weren't any good Samaritans around to help her out. The crossing guard licked the powder glaze off his fingers and daintily turned the page of his paper.

"Robyn, darling, would you make love to me right now if I told you I respect you as a mother and a businesswoman?"

She answered him by wiggling out from around him, stepping off the curb and hailing a cab. She got in without a backward glance.

Chapter Ten

"Bob McNitt, please."

"He's not here," answered a female voice with the green accent of southern Ireland. "May I ask who's calling for him?"

"Robyn. Robyn O'Halleran."

Although separated by an ocean and a sizable chunk of American soil, the ensuing silence communicated quite a bit of significance.

Robyn didn't know if it was disapproval or politeness.

"Are you by any chance Bob's mother?" Robyn asked.

"That I am."

"Are you feeling better?"

There was another long pause and then "Quite a bit better now—although my Bob was talking to a doctor on the phone last night who said that I could have a relapse at any time."

"But you're over...whatever it was you had?"

"Yes, I suppose so. For the moment. Good health is such a fragile gift. So you're Robyn."

Clutching the phone tightly, Robyn could scarcely contain her joy. Or perhaps it was a simple relief.

He must have told her.

Or maybe he was about to tell her.

She was dying to know more, but she didn't dare ask—telling his mother, or rather, asking his mother's permission to marry, was Bob's task not hers.

"Yes, I'm delighted you're doing better," she said, and then quickly apologized for interrupting Mrs McNitt's catalog of health concerns. The long-distance connection made it difficult to understand her. "Could I ask that you have Bob call me?"

"He won't be getting back for hours."

"Still, he can call me. Whatever time he gets back, I'll still be up."

After signing off, Robyn glanced at the clock and calculated the time difference.

It was after midnight at the southern tip of Ireland and Bob was generally a flip-off-the-evening-news-after-the-weather-and-go-right-to-sleep kind of guy.

But then again, he had not visited the old country in years, and his friends and family must be pulling him every which way.

She smiled as she thought of him protesting the late hour, which he was no doubt doing.

The same self-discipline that kept Bob McNitt on an early-to-bed, early-to-rise schedule had made him a success at business. Fresh out of business school, he built his own accounting business, beginning with small clients and working up to doing all the financial and tax planning for two locally owned construction companies. With the same energy and commitment he reserved for those lucrative clients, he advised young couples planning for the purchase of a home, the neighborhood grocery store putting together employee benefit programs or White Lace and Promises trying to meet its suppliers' invoices and its tax deadlines.

Bob was an older, steady, set-in-his-ways kind of guy—and Robyn appreciated that. He took things slowly—he had been her accountant for six months before he even asked her out, and then just for coffee. He liked his routine—they ate at the same neighborhood restaurant, a client of his, every Friday evening. He admitted to being uncertain about children, and he had thought her wise to not introduce him to Charlie until they were sure their own relationship was going to develop into something serious.

Although he had never married, Bob was made for married life. He was unfailingly kind and secure. He encouraged her as a businesswoman. He called when he said he would call, remembered every birthday and major holiday, didn't drink or smoke or play around. When he finally met Charlie, he developed a good relationship with him—and took him to the park on Saturdays he didn't have to meet with clients, and Charlie had brought out in him a paternal instinct that had been hidden under layers of business worries. Bob had started to talk about wanting his own children.

He hesitated about making a life commitment and here Robyn knew she had to take the initiative. It was she who told him that she loved him first—of course, once she did, he was emboldened to tell her that he felt the same way. It was she who told him that they should marry—and, after protesting that at nearly forty he was too old for her, he agreed to an engagement or at least, a pre-engagement.

It was she who told him that if he felt that his mother would appreciate the traditional act of asking permission to marry, it was all right to go to Ireland.

Alone.

Here Robyn knew she had made a mistake.

Bob's absence had made her vulnerable to Corey.

But she was protected by a small half-truth, told in a moment of panic and bewilderment at the spontaneous neighborhood party.

"Ma?"

Charlie stood in the door, wearing Pull-Ups and a T-shirt. His arms and cheeks were lightly tanned.

"Come on in, baby."

He jogged onto the bed and showed her his new action figure. Aunt Rose must have taken him to Toys "R" Us again—a nearly weekly ritual. Although Robyn always told Aunt Rose not to do it so frequently that Charlie got spoiled, she was always pleased.

After all, a trip to Toys "R" Us was a two-hour proposition between the crosstown bus ride, her son's indecision in the aisles and the long lines at the checkout counter.

Even if Robyn was officially an unwed single mother, Charlie received a lot of love.

And now there was a new father to help.

A father who wanted to marry her.

As Robyn listened with half an ear to Charlie's babbled and breathless explanation of his new toy, she studied his face. The features were so…Corey. Eyes the color of the sky. Hair as dark as ink. A strong jaw indicating an even stronger will.

"Babe magnet," she said. Charlie wrinkled his nose. "I'm just thinking you're going to be a babe magnet when you grow up. Just like your daddy."

She wasn't talking about action figures, so whatever she was saying was utterly irrelevant. But the tone of her voice was all that mattered. He rolled onto his back and lifted up his T-shirt so that she could rub his tummy.

"Song, Ma," he ordered.

She started with a Sesame Street song and kept singing until his eyes blinked and drooped and he drifted off to sleep. She had worked her way through children's songs and was trying show tunes.

"Invitation for Miss O'Halleran."

Robyn glanced up from the bed.

Corey leaned against the doorjamb, one hand shoved in the pocket of his midnight blue tuxedo pants, the other holding a bouquet of roses and a green shopping bag with the Toys "R" Us logo. His tie was undone and his hair tousled, but he made James Bond look a little scruffy.

"How long have you been standing there?" she asked, thinking of her pronounced judgment of her son's looks.

"You can come sing me a lullaby in my bed any night."

She wagged a finger at him.

He put the roses on her desk and sat on the far corner of the bed. From behind his back he produced a plastic doll wearing a faux fur tunic. It wasn't Aunt Rose who had taken Charlie shopping.

"Tarzan!" Robyn exclaimed, nearly waking Charlie. "He's been looking for that one. I even called the suburban stores. They never have it in stock when Aunt Rose takes him to the one in the city."

"They went in the back room for me. I told them you had quite a right hook and I was in fear for my life if I didn't bring a suitable peace offering."

"I'm sorry I walked out on you," she said. "It won't happen a second time. Especially if you don't get fresh with me again."

He crossed a finger over his chest.

"Scout's honor. No funny stuff. I'll wait for when you ask me to kiss you again."

"Who says I'm going to?"

"Don't get riled up. You can think 'if' if you want to. I just know it's a matter of 'when,'" he said. He ignored her stern look and reached into his suit jacket pocket for a square ecru envelope. "I said there was an invitation."

Robyn ran her finger along her engraved name.

"It's the ball this evening," Corey explained. "For the children's wing of the hospital. It was my father's charity. He gave so much for it and he was supposed to be the host this evening. I have to go in his place. I will be announcing that our old home will be turned over to the auxiliary board as a temporary dormitory for families who have children in the hospital."

Robyn opened the invitation for an eight-o'clock dinner-dance at the Ambassador West Hotel.

"You want me to go with you?"

"Separate cars seem silly."

"I can't do that," she said, putting the invitation back in the envelope. "It isn't right. I am engaged to Bob."

For a brief instance, she thought he looked as if he knew the truth. But there was no way he could.

It wasn't as if he could have talked to Bob. And no one else knew—not even Aunt Rose, in whom she usually confided.

She met his blue eyes firmly.

And the flicker of disbelief was replaced with a heavy sigh.

"It's not a memorial service," he said. "But it's the charity that he loved most, and this would have been his night. I have the notes for his speech in my pocket. Won't you come?"

"I don't think I should."

"Don't worry. I'm not going to provoke you again."

"This couldn't be a date."

"No, of course not. It's more like a tribute to my father."

"I'm an engaged woman."

He reared his head back as if any contrary assumptions were unthinkable.

"Of course. I know you'll remind me five or six times if I forget," he said. "I promise to introduce you as a friend of the family who is definitely engaged and definitely not my date."

"I don't think people need the whole intro."

"Then I'll stick with f.o.f."

"What happened to acting unethically?"

"I'm taking a break for the night."

"You could be lying, and if you were unethical, you would tell me right now that you weren't."

"And if I was acting with aboveboard honesty and forthrightness, I would say the same thing."

"I'd better not go."

"Robyn, the thing is that my acting unethically won't work if you're committed to being engaged. It takes two people to cheat on Bob. Are you worried that you're not really committed to him? I mean, how strong is your love for him? If it can't survive going to a dinner-dance meant to honor my father..."

Robyn's hackles rose.

"All right. I'll go if Aunt Rose can baby-sit. But I'm not sure I have anything to wear."

He raised an eyebrow.

"You make gowns for a living, and you don't have one or two or a hundred dresses stashed away for yourself?"

"No, I don't have any need for finery, after-hours clothes."

"Bob doesn't take you..." He caught her warning glance. "Okay, okay, just wear what you have on."

She looked down at her worn-out jeans and the white pocket T-shirt.

"I'll find something," she said, sliding her arm out from under Charlie. "Watch him."

She went downstairs to the shop, thinking that there might be a returned dress hidden away. Very few women brought back a gown to White Lace and Promises but when they did, Robyn was generous about returning their money, even if the gown was made to the client's specifications. Robyn had always figured that a canceled wedding or being stood up for the prom was horrible enough without having to pay for a dress.

Aunt Rose sat at her long table, threading a needle in the light of the setting sun. In front of her was a simple sheath made from the finest white silk they had imported from India the month before. Although it looked like a primitively constructed rectangle, Robyn knew all Aunt Rose's work contained flattering deceptions of cut and line that made a woman look her best.

"Try it on," Aunt Rose said, clipping a knotted thread.

Robyn picked up the dress by its shoulders.

"It's so beautiful. How did you know I'd need a dress?"

"I know only what all women know," Aunt Rose said, snapping the lid shut on her sewing basket. "There is something special about a woman in white. Something that no man can resist."

"I don't want to make myself irresistible to Corey."

"You want," Aunt Rose said. "You just don't want to admit it. To yourself or anyone else."

"I'm marrying Bob," Robyn said, putting the dress down. "You liked him."

"I like him fine. But Corey's your son's father."

"That's not enough to make a marriage."

Aunt Rose stared heavenward.

"It was good enough in my time. Now, Robyn O'Halleran, you can thank me now or you can thank me later for the dress."

"Thank you now," Robyn said, remembering her manners. She put an arm around her aunt's birdlike shoulders. "Thank you."

"And here's a pair of matching shoes. I hope your feet are still the same size."

Aunt Rose handed her a plastic-lined red silk shoe bag. Robyn pulled out the pale *peau de soie* slippers.

"These are the ones I wore to the debutante ball."

"I kept them."

On one of them was the faintest smudge.

She remembered her nervousness the night of the ball. How she had jumped from the limousine, determined to get on with the party, with her life. Rushing headlong through traffic and losing her shoe in a pothole.

Whenever she thought of the ball, she always remembered her shoes. How the lesson of losing her slipper was that she had to put the brakes on herself. Reason through her choices. Act responsibly. Take things slowly.

Otherwise, more than shoes would be ruined.

But, holding the slipper, all she could think of was the magic of her Prince Charming's touch on her ankle as he came to her rescue.

She showered and talced herself in the bathroom. Then she tried on the dress. The fabric tugged at her breasts just so. But the magic of a white dress by Aunt Rose was undeniable. She knew it when she opened the bedroom door and, after a moment of watching Charlie and Corey playing with Tarzan, she asked if Corey was ready. He glanced at her and then could not take his eyes away.

"Wow," he said, rising to his feet.

"That's what you said the first time you saw me in white," Robyn said, feeling unaccountably pleased to have rendered him nearly speechless.

"I meant it four years ago, and I mean it today," Corey said.

Charlie, toting the Tarzan figure in his hand, slid down from the bed and ran to her. She picked him up.

"Pwetty," he declared, tugging a damp, dark red curl. "Pwetty."

She kissed her boy and stared over his head at Corey, meeting his stare with one of equal intensity, equal challenge, and though she would never admit to it, equal interest.

"Shall we go?" he said at last.

She nodded.

"I just need to get my bag and stop downstairs."

Aunt Rose walked up behind her and took Charlie. "Say goodbye to Mommy and Daddy," she said. "We're having our own party tonight."

"Ma," Charlie said, holding his hand up and wiggling his fingers. "Cow-ee."

"Daddy," Corey corrected.

"Cow-ee."

"Daddy."

Charlie giggled. Corey took Robyn's arm. When they reached the bottom of the stairs, Charlie shrieked and said, "Cow-ee!"

"Give it up," Aunt Rose advised. "He'll make you his daddy when he chooses."

Corey figured he'd give Charlie a lesson on daddies later, because something else had caught his attention. Robyn had taken an inch-wide organdy ribbon and a handful of velvet lilies of the valley and had pulled her curls into a gentle ponytail that trailed all the way down her back.

Actresses. Models. Socialites. Heiresses. Even a princess and a duchess or two. Corey Harte had gone out with women who were supposed to be beauties, and some deserved the public assessment while others were the products of dogged publicists, skilled stylists and tremendous hype.

But he knew he was a lucky man tonight. He was going out with a true beauty. The little girl who had moved with her mother into the carriage house behind his home. The little girl who always went to him with her scraped knees. The woman who had given him her first and only lovemaking. The mother of his child. And if he played this gamble through to the end, his wife.

Chapter Eleven

The hospital had rented a car to bring Dr. Harte to its benefit. The black stretch limousine glided gently through Thursday-evening rush-hour traffic backed up on Lake Shore Drive. In the back seat, Robyn accepted a flute of champagne from Corey.

"To my father and to our future as..." Corey said, tapping his glass to hers.

"Parents," Robyn said firmly. "Simply parents."

"Parents," Corey conceded.

She took a tiny sip, letting the ice-cold bubbles explode in her mouth.

"I wonder if it was wrong of me to never contact your father," she said, looking out on the lake where Corey had scattered his father's ashes. "Perhaps I should have let him meet Charlie."

"I talked to Walter today, and he said he had spent yesterday evening going through Dad's papers. He found some pictures of Charlie," Corey said. "Looked like they were taken at a park, possibly through telephoto lens. He had hired a private detective to keep tabs. His way of keeping close but not interfering. I just don't know why he didn't tell me."

Robyn put her glass down in the circular holder at her armrest. She took Corey's hand in her own and squeezed gently.

"I was the one who decided not to have any relationship with you or your father," she said. "Your father was respecting my decision even as he made sure that when he died you would know you had a son."

"I should have been told," Corey said mildly. "By you or by him. I would have done things differently. I would have taken a residency here. Or taken an easier study course so that we could have married."

"You would have done what you're trying to do now. Marry me to give your son your name and your family."

"Charlie's not the only reason we should marry."

"Well, there's no way of ever finding that out, is there?"

"No, I guess there isn't. Because if I told you right now that I love you, you'd say I was just doing whatever was necessary."

Robyn pulled her hand out from his grip.

"That's right."

"And if I told you I had thought that night that we would marry—someday—but just not then, it wouldn't be enough to change your mind about me, would it?"

"It wouldn't make any difference. I was mad at you, and I let my pride get in the way. But later, weeks later, when I found out I was pregnant, I was thinking clearly. I did the right thing. Or at least, I did what I thought was right."

He ran his fingers through his hair.

"Robyn, just for tonight, let's forget the past. And even the present. Let's just be who we are. The day after tomorrow is Saturday. You'll be getting married."

"To Bob."

"If that's what you want. But give me this night. Just this night. Without reminding me of the man who's taking my place in Charlie's life. And yours."

"I said it wasn't a date."

"This isn't. It's a friend of the family going out with a friend from another family."

"What's the difference?"

"Just this."

She thought he was going to kiss her. And then she'd have to tell him to stop. Or, at least, she *should* tell him to stop.

But he made no attempt at that intimacy. Instead, he took her hand, entwined her fingers in his own and squeezed ever so gently. And then he let go of her fingers. Each one of them felt naked and exposed.

He took his champagne glass and sipped, commenting benignly about the weather or the news or maybe it was traffic.

Robyn didn't know. Because Robyn had just felt somehow rebuffed. He hadn't kissed her. He was supposed to try to kiss her. And if he didn't try to kiss her, he was at least supposed to tell her something along the lines of *You want me, Robyn O'Halleran. Oh, yes, you do.*

But he didn't.

Good.

Because he shouldn't.

She had said he shouldn't.

Because she had spent four years outgrowing him, learning to think with her head instead of her heart, learning to be responsible and clear thinking.

So why was she feeling somehow bereft?

With a somewhat muddled satisfaction, she leaned back in her seat, drank a little champagne, watched the backup of traffic heading toward the northern suburbs, checked her evening bag for the portable phone that Aunt Rose would call if there were any emergencies.

Or if Bob were to call.

And then, as if possessing a mind of its own, her hand dropped to the space on the seat between them, open palm up.

Corey did not look at her.

Did not even glance her way.

Did not miss a beat in his soliloquy on the vagaries of Chicago weather.

Did not even pounce or gloat or revel in this small victory.

Instead, he placed his hand on hers, and without acknowledgment by either of them, they held hands until the limousine pulled to a stop before the green-tasseled awning of the Ambassador West Hotel. As the driver opened their door, a short, squat man wearing black plastic-framed glasses and a houndstooth jacket shoved a camera toward the couple and took three shots in rapid succession.

Robyn jerked her hand back onto her lap.

"Aw, Rusty, stop that right now," Corey said, alighting from the car and turning to help Robyn out. "Put the camera away."

"You're in an uncooperative mood tonight," Rusty observed. "And who's the dame?"

"Friend of the family," Corey said.

Rusty looked Robyn up and down.

"I got lots of friends of my family and none of them look like this," he said. He darted around Corey to take another shot of Robyn. "So who are you?"

"Friend of the family," Robyn repeated, following Corey's lead into the hotel.

"Wait a minute! I remember you. The housekeeper's daughter who became a deb."

A bell captain stepped in to block Rusty's path when he tried to follow them.

"Must be pretty serious," he called out. "'Cause I don't know any women who aren't pleased as punch to get their picture taken with C.M.E.B." He looked up the chest of the dour-faced captain. "An Andrew Jackson if you let me in."

The bell captain laughed, indicating that twenty bucks wouldn't get him to move an inch, much less let Rusty into the swank hotel.

THE FRIEND of the Harte family was introduced to everyone at the receiving line, and many people recalled the striking redhead who had been a swan among the nice but nonetheless duckling debutante class of four years before.

Someone asked their escort if the friend of the family was the redhead who had starred in the French film they had seen in Cannes.

Overhearing the question, the stockbroker standing behind them in the receiving line told his wife that the f.o.f. was definitely the redhead in the movie from Cannes—but nobody in the foursome behind the stockbroker could remember the film's title much less the plot.

Standing behind the foursome in the line stretching out of the hotel ballroom, Ashford Pinksmith III said no, she was a debutante that he had escorted four years before, and she had been a delightful girl, although not nearly as delightful as Lelaine Paik—whom he had met that very same night.

"Yeah, right, she was with you," Lelaine said, lightly punching his arm. "Ashford, you've been going to debutante balls so long you can't remember the women you've escorted."

At the head of the line, Robyn stood at Corey's side, welcoming guests to the dinner.

"I run a dress shop," Robyn corrected gently, when one grand dame asked her what it was like working with the French director who was rumored to be "artistically difficult."

The old woman fingered the fabric of Robyn's dress approvingly.

"Did this dress come from your shop?"

"Yes."

"Who was the designer? No, let me guess. Mizrahi? Beene? No, it must be an Armani."

"Aunt Rose."

"I've heard of Aunt Rose," the woman sniffed approvingly. "An English company. Well-made dresses that last a lifetime. I've even bought a few of their gowns in my day. Give me your card. The party season is just beginning, and my closet looks so dreary."

"Ma'am, Aunt Rose is my aunt."

"Oh, really? That must be quite nice having such a famous relation."

When the waiter walked through the cocktail

hall, ringing the delicate crystal dinner bell, Robyn O'Halleran hadn't a single business card left, and she had several appointments lined up for the next week.

"You're so at ease," Corey marveled, slipping his hand under her elbow. He escorted her to the head table.

"I'm not really, but when there's a possibility of new clients for White Lace and Promises, I can do a pretty good imitation of someone who fits in."

"You fit in fine. You're my—"

"Friend of the family."

"I never said anything to the contrary."

He helped her into her seat and then took his place at the podium. When the guests settled down, he brought out his notes. But he set them aside, at a corner of the podium, and spoke directly from the heart. About his father, his father's legacy at the hospital, of the love he had felt for the children who came for treatment.

He announced the donation of the home he had grown up in, and was met with thunderous applause. Though he had women—and a few men— dabbing their eyes with their handkerchiefs, he concluded with a humorous anecdote about his father that left the partygoers in a very good mood.

A festive mood that was the highest tribute to the late Dr. Harte.

"You look pretty at ease yourself," Robyn said

to him as he returned to the table amidst a standing ovation.

"I'm not really, any more than you are, but it's for my father's charity so I try my best. We'll raise even more money for the children's wing tonight."

He tapped his champagne flute against hers.

"Business is over. Now it's our time."

Later she would say that here was where she had made her mistake. She should have reminded him that she was only here because this was the only memorial to his father that she could attend. That they could be friends, good friends, who raised a son together, but anything further was a mistake.

But she didn't say any of that.

Ordinarily Chicago society vied for the opportunity to speak with young Dr. Harte, and a mysterious beauty is always cause for jostling—for a word, a glance, a smile. The letter of the laws of etiquette require conversational focus to shift with every course, but the spirit of etiquette allows for magical exceptions.

The banker on Robyn's right became so engrossed in the mortgage travails of the woman to his right that he scarcely had a word for Robyn through soup, salad, entrée, dessert and even the after-dinner coffee.

The woman on Corey's left had just had dental surgery that had taken two hours, and her description required three. The orthodontic surgeon on her left was a professional rival to her dentist, so he nodded and bleated sympathetically at every gory detail. Corey was free to spend his time focused on the woman he loved.

Over a salad of roasted peppers, blue cheese and arugula, Corey told Robyn about his residency, and while none of his comments contained a single boast or conceit, Robyn knew enough to recognize a hero of the emergency room. As waiters placed the orange-glazed chicken they would barely touch in front of them, Corey directed the talk to Robyn and the past four years. He was admiring, but not totally surprised at how she had fought to make White Lace and Promises a profitable business while reserving most of her energy for Charlie.

"You've really grown up," he said, squeezing her hand. And catching her familiar bristle, he said, "I'm admiring you—not pointing out how I'm taller or faster or smarter or older."

"Then you've done some growing up, too!"

And they both laughed.

While they had both grown in the past four years, nonetheless they had gone in the same direction. Both had taken responsibility for others. Both had lost a certain brashness. Both had mastered their crafts—medicine, motherhood and business.

And both had carried inside a powerful, aching loneliness that they had squelched and ignored, a loneliness that only this magical evening had ever relieved.

The last bites of chocolate and puff pastry were eaten. The men, following the lead of the guests seated at the head table, rose from their seats to ask their dinner partners to dance.

The banker, who was, strictly speaking, required to ask for Robyn's first dance—announced he was too tired. The woman who had endured dental surgery declined Corey's polite request because she said the pain medication made her woozy.

"Robyn, I guess it's just you and me," Corey said.

And even in the crowded ballroom, it was just Robyn and Corey.

He led her to the tiger maple parquet floor and put his arms around her just as the orchestra opened with a slow and sentimental tune. Corey laid his hand against the small of her back, and she gently placed a hand on his shoulder.

He was a good dancer, mandatory lessons had taken care of that, but he was dancing for pleasure now. And dancing was really only an opportunity to touch Robyn, to feel her body against his, to smell her clean scent of lily of the valley and talc.

And feeling this good with Robyn was what made Corey a perfect dancer.

After two sets, the orchestra shifted its mood—adding tunes that were brighter and more modern. Just the sort of thing that Corey and Robyn should appreciate...but they didn't.

They looked at each other, between them hanging the question of What now?

It was wrong. She shouldn't. She had been down this path once and had made a mistake—a mistake that had given her the greatest blessing of her life but one that she shouldn't repeat.

But his hand had slipped to her hip. His scent, enduringly masculine, intoxicated her.

"Let's go home," she said, feeling the history of her life repeat itself and being utterly powerless to stop herself when he touched her.

Chapter Twelve

As if fearing that she'd change her mind, he held on to her hand, made quick and perfunctory good-byes to a few of his colleagues and led her through the mahogany-and-velvet lobby.

Their driver had somehow guessed that they would want to leave early, and the sleek black limousine pulled up to the awning just as they stepped onto the sidewalk. Corey followed her into the back seat and, after instructing the driver to go to his Astor Street address, slid the opaque screen up for total privacy.

"Come here, baby," he said. "I've been waiting for years."

Robyn came to him, climbing onto his lap, one foot dangling off the edge of the seat. He took her face in his hands and sighed.

"Sorry, I can't kiss you till you ask me."

"I'm asking," Robyn said hoarsely. "Please, I'm asking."

And she kissed him.

She had waited so long that the first brush of her lips against his had the faintly wistful quality of recollection. His lips tasted something like berries, but berries was not what made her so hungry for more. Her mouth opened to him. His tongue touched the cool, smooth surface of her teeth.

And the kiss became something better than memory, finer than any dream.

She wanted him, had to have him, had used up all her reasons to deny him and so was left with nothing but desire. She straddled him, slipping her hands into his suit jacket so that she could explore the lattice of muscles running from his chest to his taut abdomen.

She felt his hands grasp her breasts and she flung back her head with a ripple of pleasure from her throat. He kissed the exposed flesh, hearing her moan from hunger—it had truly been four years without touch.

When he stopped, when he pulled the shoulder of her dress back up to its innocent perch, when he pulled his tie back in order, she thought: *No!* But the limousine came to a stop at the curb and the driver opened the door as Robyn slid her feet back into her shoes and corralled her hair into a semblance of order.

"Go open the door," Corey suggested, handing her his key.

She slipped past the driver, who kept his eyes discreetly lowered.

Corey tipped the driver and dismissed him. Robyn walked through the canopy of parkway trees to a cobblestone sidewalk in front of his home. Corey stepped up behind her.

"Shall we go in?" he asked, and slipped the key from her fingers. He trotted up the granite steps. "Are you coming?"

"Yes...I mean, no."

His eyebrows came together.

"What's the matter?"

"I can't, Corey. I just can't," she said, wishing there was more than a streetlight to illuminate his expression. Would he be angry that she had pulled him out of that party simply to tell him—

"Robyn, you don't have to do anything you don't want to."

"I want to. But I can't. Please don't be mad at me."

"I'm not mad, but is this about Bob? Because I know a few things about Bob and..."

"Don't call him a mouse again," she warned, trailing her hand along the delicate wrought-iron fence that surrounded a bed of voluptuous ferns. "It's not him. It's me."

Corey sat on the top step and swept the errant leaves and twigs away.

"Sit here beside me and tell me about you."

She stepped neither forward nor back—instead she worried an acorn finial on the gate.

"I rush into things," she explained. "I rush into things not thinking about how they'll turn out."

"Give me an example."

"Remember when I got impatient with the traffic on the night of the ball? Remember how I ran?"

"I remember that the limousine Ashford rented wouldn't have dropped you off until after midnight."

"I ruined my shoe on a pothole," she said, poking her slipper out from under her dress and regarding the dark smudge ruefully. "And it was all because I didn't stop and think about the consequences of my actions."

"What happened to your shoe is what you think about the magic that happened between us that night?"

"A little," she said.

"Robyn, you can't carefully weigh the costs and benefits of falling in love. You can't decide that it's a wise idea or poor planning to feel passion. You can't make a list of the good points and bad points of the man you love. It's not how the heart works."

"It's how my heart works," she said firmly. "I'm not impulsive now. I look before I leap. I have to—I have a child, a business, an aunt to look after."

He stood up. "What do I have to do to persuade you that I'm the wisest option?"

"I don't know. I don't think you can."

"Are you going to marry Bob before you give me a chance?"

"He's coming back Saturday. I've built a relationship with him. I won't throw it away."

He nodded and took her hand. "I won't invite you in, because one of us would do something foolish," he said.

"Why don't you take me home?" she said. "We have a lot to think about."

ROBYN UNLOCKED the shop with her key.

"Wait here. I'll turn off the security alarm," she said. She ran to the keypad at the back of the storeroom just as she heard a telephone ring. She punched in the disarming code and went back into the front room.

"It's a patient," Corey mouthed as he held the phone to his ear. "I left this number in case my beeper didn't work."

Robyn nodded and pantomimed that she'd be upstairs making coffee. Corey held up a finger indicating he'd like a cup, too.

"The cough sounds suspicious," Corey was saying as Robyn's footsteps receded. "I'd recommend complete bed rest, plenty of fluids and stress reduction. Stress can be caused by great happiness or sadness—don't start any family discussions. As your doctor, I'd like to see her on a completely even keel.''

He listened, nodding absently and then shook his head vigorously.

''Bob, please, don't worry about Robyn. She was talking just today about how rushing into things is always a mistake. I'm sure she was referring to how you're going to talk to your mom about the wedding.''

After a few minutes of reassurance, Corey told Bob good-night and walked upstairs.

''So do you have to go to the hospital?'' Robyn asked, taking some peanut butter cookies from a tin on the counter. She arranged them on two plates.

''No, the patient just needed a little soothing,'' Corey said, loosening his tie. ''Robyn, you're not going to make me walk back out into the cold, dark night, are you?''

''It's not cold—it's an unusually warm April. And it's not dark—there's streetlights at every corner. But you can use the couch.''

''Where are you going? Aren't we going to have coffee together?''

''The coffee's for you,'' Robyn said, walking down the hall. She stopped and picked up a teddy bear and put it in bed with Charlie in the little alcove. ''I'm just in it for the cookies. Good night!''

GOOD POINTS:
healthy
work out regularly
have a good job with benefits
make monthly deposits in a savings account
own my own home
am a good father—experience to follow
don't drink to excess
don't smoke or take drugs
will be monogamous
  BAD POINTS:

Rubbing his smooth jaw, Corey studied the white sheet of paper which he had divided into two columns.

"I drink milk and orange juice directly from the carton," he concluded. "Unless someone's there to tell me not to."

Can be trained on domestic matters, he wrote on the left side of the page.

Still didn't solve the problem of the snowy white right side of the page.

"Try arrogant, conceited and unwilling to consider that other people might have a better idea," Robyn said, leaning over his shoulder.

He glanced up from her kitchen table. She was still in her pajamas, with her hair in a bed-ready dishevelment that stylists spent hours trying to reproduce for catalog models.

"Okay," he said. And wrote *confident* and *decisive* and *sexy?* on the left side of the page.

"Corey!"

"I'm trying to do this your way," he said. "The rational, logical, don't-step-into-any-potholes way. I've been sitting here since you went to sleep listing my qualities as a potential husband."

"You didn't get any sleep?"

"I'm a doctor. I'm trained to overcome tiredness. Which reminds me..." He wrote *high energy* in the left-hand column. He was pleased to note that she didn't look as though she had gotten any more sleep than he had. Lack of sleep wore down many a young doctor-in-training—she wouldn't be any different. "I did Bob's list. Wanna see it?"

"No."

He pulled out the paper underneath his pad. The left side was blank. But the right side was filled to the margins.

"Bad Points: Mama's boy, cheap, boring, too old for you, cold fish in bed..."

"Corey!"

"Well, he must not be very sexy."

"You have no idea."

"I might not, but you don't have any contrary evidence."

She glared.

"I'm going to marry you, Robyn," he said confidently.

She poured herself a cup of coffee and sat across from him.

"Why?"

"Because I'm a healthy male who works out regularly, has a good job with benefits—"

"No, I mean why do you want to marry me?"

"Because I'm Charlie's dad."

"Exactly. That's not enough for me," she said. "You know, I didn't make the decision to marry Bob lightly. I took a lot of time…"

"What if Bob weren't coming back on Saturday?"

She narrowed her eyes dangerously. "He's coming back on Saturday."

"Just what if he weren't? What if something happened and he felt he had to stay in Ireland a little longer?"

"I would fly to Ireland," she said, rising to her feet. "Because whatever would happen to keep him there would be important enough for me to help him."

"Would you take Charlie?"

She looked suspicious and she should be. He worked his best magic with wide blue eyes and an innocent expression.

"I'd take Charlie and Aunt Rose," Robyn said. "Charlie's never been to Ireland, and Aunt Rose would dearly love to see the rest of the family. Which reminds me, maybe I should call Ireland again, because I haven't heard from him. Maybe his mother forgot to tell him I called.''

OPERATION COURTSHIP officially began as soon as Aunt Rose woke up.

"Here, I need your help," Corey said, handing her a cup of coffee as soon as she came into the kitchen.

"Last night?"

He shook his head.

"Oh, dear."

She sat at the table and glanced sidelong at his lists.

"That's not how you do it, Corey."

"Obviously," he said, crumpling the paper and tossing it across the kitchen into the trash.

"You have a lot of success with women, right?"

"I guess," he said, shrugging uncomfortably.

"Oh, Corey, of course you do. Nothing to be embarrassed about. You've had enough success that you've never had to work at it. But what do you think most women notice first about you?"

He ducked his head.

"I don't know."

"Your name?"

He considered the fact that his name, long associated with wealth and prestige, had opened many doors. Including bedroom doors.

"I suppose," he conceded.

"Well, she's grown up with the Harte name all

her life. She's not impressed. What about your wealth? Are women drawn to that?''

''Some, I suppose.''

''Most, I'd imagine! She doesn't care about your wallet. She started off scared and uncertain—but that girl developed a head for business. She makes her own money. She won't put up with a slacker, but she's not looking for a man to support her. What about your looks?''

''What about them?''

''Do women find you handsome?''

He shifted in his chair.

''I'll answer that one for you,'' Aunt Rose said. ''They do. But while that'll get you an invitation to a few bedrooms, it won't open Robyn's door.''

''So what's left?''

Aunt Rose pointed to his chest.

''Your heart. That's all that's left, Corey. Your heart.''

''I STILL DON'T SEE why I had to try it on,'' Robyn said, regarding herself in the mirror. The dress she had worn to her debutante ball tugged a little tighter at her breasts and draped a little more provocatively from her hips.

''We need a wedding dress,'' Corey said, amending his statement when she flashed him a look. ''You need a wedding dress. I'm just thinking of Bob. He'd like a pretty bride.''

He had spent the day in surgery and had come

to the apartment so beat looking that Robyn hadn't had the heart to remind him that he didn't live with them. He lay stretched out on top of the bed with his head propped up on his elbow.

He was fully dressed and lying over not under the sheets, and yet, looking so sexy that Robyn glanced over at Aunt Rose to see if she noticed.

Aunt Rose spared not a glance for Corey. She tugged a dainty embroidered handkerchief from the pocket of her sundress.

"You look just as lovely as you did four years ago," she exclaimed. "A regular angel, you are."

"Don't either of you think it's a little creepy to wear this dress? If I'm marrying Bob, it's just a reminder of…"

"No!" Corey and Aunt Rose said in unison.

"Besides, Bob'll like the fact that the dress doesn't cost anything," Corey added.

"Stand still," Aunt Rose said, opening her sewing basket on the desk. "Stop glaring at him—it'll give you wrinkles on your forehead before your time. I've got to fix the shoulder. Just stand right there. Don't move. It'll just take three stitches."

Robyn looked at the phone as Aunt Rose worked. She had called so many times to Ireland, she knew she was annoying Bob's mother. But he was never home. So many relatives, so many long-lost friends—forget the wedding, poor Bob was going to need a few days' rest when he came back just to recover from the trip.

And he had to come back Saturday. He just had to come back.

"Stop tapping your foot, young lady," Aunt Rose said. "Makes it so I can't concentrate. By the way, did I tell you that Charlie and I are going to sleep over at Marge's house tonight? Her grandson is coming, and you know how those two like to play."

"Sure," Robyn said. Aunt Rose's bridge partner Marge had come over the previous month with her grandson, and the sleepover was a great success. "Just as long as Corey knows that he's not..."

She glanced over at the bed. Corey had fallen asleep.

Aunt Rose bit the thread off and patted Robyn's back.

"Don't you dare wake that man up," she ordered. "He saved a child's life on the operating table this afternoon, and I think that entitles him to a bit o' rest."

"Aunt Rose..."

Aunt Rose gathered her sewing supplies and dumped them into her basket.

"Aunt Rose, he can't stay here..."

Aunt Rose called to Charlie, who sat on the living room couch with his backpack already on his shoulders.

"Aunt Rose, I will not stand for this..."

Charlie was instructed by his aunt to blow his mother a kiss goodbye, which he did.

"Aunt Rose, you can't leave me alone with this man in this apartment."

"And why not?" Aunt Rose asked, putting a snug cloche on her head.

"Because something might happen!"

"Then perhaps you should go out," Aunt Rose advised, calmly taking Charlie's hand. "But you don't wake that man until he's ready to get up. Ta!"

Robyn stared at the freshly slammed door.

Stuck in an apartment with Corey.

Trouble surely to follow.

If he wasn't going out, maybe she should. Go out, that is.

Plenty of things to do, Robyn thought as she heard the downstairs door of the shop close behind Aunt Rose and Charlie.

Grocery shopping.

Making a deposit at the cash machine.

Books to be returned to the library.

She reached behind to unzip the dress as she wondered whether the videos Aunt Rose rented the previous weekend had been returned.

That's when she noticed.

She flew to the window, pulled up the sash, and shouted, "You sewed my zipper shut!"

Aunt Rose paused at the streetlight, letting go of Charlie's hand only long enough to raise a plaintive plea to heaven.

"Sorry. Must be my arthritis," she said with

good-natured contrition. "See you tomorrow morning."

"Aunt Rose, you don't even have arthritis!" Robyn said, shoving the window closed.

She walked back to the bedroom, held her hand poised to wake him and then thought of the child who had been rushed to Corey's hospital, pulled from the wreckage of a five-car pileup.

She stood for several minutes, listening to his rhythmic breathing.

Coming closer, she pushed a lock of glossy hair back from his forehead. He looked so peaceful and so harmless and she was so very tired that she almost lay down beside him.

No, she thought, glancing at the nightstand picture of her soon-to-be husband.

Impulse is trouble. Clear-headed, rational thinking the only salvation. Sleeping next to Corey would be wrong. Very wrong. He might be immobilized by sleep, but he would awaken and there would be trouble.

"Sorry, Bob," she said.

Then, deciding that she couldn't very well go on her errands wearing a formal gown, she sat for the long vigil in the living room with a pair of sheathed sewing scissors clasped in her hand.

Chapter Thirteen

She was only mildly aware of the feel of the crocheted antimacassar pressed against her cheek, slightly more aware of the smell of home cooking, gradually aware that someone was watching her.

And that someone was Corey.

She bolted upright in the armchair.

"Were you waiting to kill me with these?" he asked, holding up the scissors.

"No, I need you to cut a seam," Robyn said groggily. "What time is it?"

"Eight o'clock."

"How long have you been awake?"

"A few hours. Where's the seam?"

She stood up, rubbed her eyes and turned around.

"Aunt Rose sewed the zipper together. I can't unzip the dress, and if I pull it, it'll rip apart. So cut the stitches. Then you can go home."

"No."

She jerked her head around. "What?"

"No. Dinner first. I made spaghetti. Then I'll help you."

"Give me those scissors. Did you tell Aunt Rose to do this?"

"No, but I'm mighty grateful she did."

Robyn snatched the scissors and went to her bedroom. She stood in front of the mirror. Tried it right-handed from the bottom.

"You've got some lace caught," Corey said, sauntering into the mirror's reflection.

Robyn tried it from the top.

"You're digging into the fabric."

She glared.

"Dinner," Corey offered. "Then I'll cut it."

"And go right home. I'm serious, Corey. There can be nothing between us. Tomorrow I'm marrying Bob. I'm engaged, you know."

She put the scissors on the desk.

"Dinner, Mrs. Soon-To-Be-McNitt," he conceded. "Just dinner."

DINNER WASN'T something fancy, wasn't something elegant, wasn't something that would get its chef on the cover of *Gourmet Life*. It was just...dinner. A plate of spaghetti, a tossed salad and soda in plastic glasses—thrown together with things he had found in the refrigerator and cabinets.

But it was a good dinner, and Corey noted that

she seemed more comfortable with him once he promised to go home.

A promise he knew he would break.

He worked from a sophisticated knowledge base that Robyn just didn't possess.

It wasn't fair.

It wasn't nice.

It wasn't ethical.

It was taking advantage of an innocent woman—something he would disapprove of in any other man, with any other woman, in any other situation.

But ethics had flown out the window.

He used all the tricks of seduction, but he was subtle, so very subtle, with his conversation, with the covert compliment, the heavy-lidded glance that when he cleared the plates she handed him the scissors only when he reminded her.

"Snip it and go home," she said, her lower lip trembling.

She stood in the center of the kitchen floor, her head bowed, her hand holding her hair up to expose her nape.

He touched her flesh. And the baby-fine down at her hairline rose to meet his fingertips.

"You're not kissing me, are you?"

"Should I?"

"No, of course not."

"Time for me to go," he said, snipping one of the criss-crossed stitches that held the zipper shut.

"Time for me to leave you," he snipped another and another. "Time for us to say goodbye."

She turned around just as he finished his work.

"Are you sure you want to go?" she asked in a quavering voice.

"I think I'll stay for dessert."

He picked her up and strode to her bedroom.

"Take your dress off first. I don't want to rip it again."

"That seems a little cold just to order me to—"

He put her down. "You take off the dress, I'll take off this."

He slipped off his jacket, yanked his tie out of his collar band and popped the buttons off his shirt. His chest was broad and muscular. It was all Robyn could do not to reach out and touch him, to spread her hands out along the rich, dark curl of hair that came to a single line leading to the pants button that he was just undoing.

"You're not taking off your dress," he observed.

She backed off so that she was standing on the other side of the bed.

"I have to tell you something first," she said.

"What?"

"I did something very wrong. I've never told you. I guess because I was so embarrassed and even ashamed. And now that we're here—" she gestured to the bed which seemed suddenly very

large and not so innocently quilted "—I have to
talk to you about it again."

"What is it?"

"Birth control."

"I've come prepared."

"It's not about now. It's about then…"

"I've figured it out, Robyn," he said, and he
took off his shirt. "But I still want you to take off
your dress."

"Just so that we're clear—I told you I was, but
I wasn't."

"And you've been feeling guilty all this time?"

"A little. All right, a lot. I was so foolish to
think nothing would happen my first time. It's part
of why I thought it was unfair for you to know.
About Charlie."

"Every time a man makes love, he takes the risk
that he's making a baby. If he doesn't want a baby
with that woman, he has no right to make love to
her."

"That's a very enlightened statement coming
from the C.M.E.B."

"It's how I feel," he said. "Now, before I rip
Aunt Rose's handiwork from collar to hem, would
you take the damn dress off?"

"Why, Corey, you have the most romantic way
about you," Robyn said smartly.

She pulled the dress up over her head, and when
she brought her arms down she had Corey in her
embrace. He nuzzled her shoulder, drew his head

down to her breasts and greedily sucked on each nipple as he unclasped her bra. She thought she could not stand it anymore, the sensation that eclipsed reason, but as she pulled a stockinged leg up to rub against him, she knew she was going higher.

"Come here, baby," he murmured, and laid her gently upon the bed. "Let me love you."

He was so gentle, so very gentle, that she didn't notice how he reached for the nightstand, and as he switched off the light, turned down the picture of Bob.

So gentle that when he clasped her hands up over her head so that she arched for his appraisal, she didn't notice the ring that Bob had given her slip from her fingers into the palm of his hand.

So gentle that when he slipped into her she felt only the contractions of awakened pleasure and his name repeated on her lips. That gentleness was only broken by his climax, the pulse driving into her as she urged him yes, yes and again yes.

"COREY, I FEEL terrible," she said. "Don't you feel terrible?"

"No," he murmured at her shoulder. "I feel wonderful. What I can't figure out is how you could feel terrible."

"I cheated. On Bob."

"Hush! Don't worry about that."

"We're...engaged."

"It'll get sorted out."

"I thought you had an honor system where you wouldn't poach another man's woman."

"Yeah, well, call me unethical."

"If you're unethical, I don't even want to think what I am."

"I'll marry you, even if you're unfaithful to Bob."

"I'm going to have to call him tomorrow morning. And tell him."

"Tomorrow's today. It's nearly two o'clock in the morning. Don't turn your head away. I want you again."

"But don't you feel guilty?"

"I'm feeling something…but it's not guilt."

Later she had to sleep. She just didn't have Corey's stamina. As she drifted off, she knew she had a lot of difficult things ahead of her—explaining this to Bob was not going to be easy—but she had no doubts, no doubts at all that she was Corey's woman. She could not deny that.

Did he love her?

She closed her eyes. Felt Corey's body next to hers. His arm thrown over her stomach.

Bob.

Somehow her thoughts kept drifting back to Bob.

Bob.

Somehow she kept hearing the name.

She had cheated on him. Cheated on Bob. It was wrong.

She was just as unethical as Corey.

But now she couldn't get Bob's name out of her head.

Did it mean she had traded her previous future of lusting after one man, yet settling down with another, for living in a state of lustful surrender to Corey while relinquishing the steadiness of…

Bob.

Bob.

Bob.

"BOB, BOB, SHUT UP and listen to me. She's fine," Corey said. He had picked up the nightstand phone on the first ring, assuming incorrectly it was his service with a patient emergency. But when he heard the long-distance whine, he knew. "Calm down. You take your time, don't rush telling your mother."

He listened and nodded, nodded and listened.

"I'm a doctor—and I'm telling you your mom's cold could return at any moment. Stress, even the happy stress of finding out her son is getting married, is definitely a factor in a relapse. And a relapse could be…I don't even want to say how bad it could be."

He glanced over at Robyn. She was stirring.

"Bob, I've got, uh, an emergency operation I

have to perform. My advice—don't tell your mom yet. The shock will be too much.''

Robyn was turning over, but her luxurious curls covered the part of her face that moonlight would have illuminated. Was she awake?

"Don't worry about Robyn," he said, rushing his words, trying to get Bob to sign off. "I'll take care of telling her."

Robyn sat up straight. She should be looking at him lovingly, but for some reason she wasn't.

"I'll break it to her gently," he said.

She stood up, caught his admiring eye, covered herself with a flannel night dress. So that her breasts were barely visible over the top of the fabric, which was actually the hem of the gown.

She looked angry. Definitely angry.

Even illuminated only by the corner streetlight, he could see it.

"Hear that, Bob? It's my patient calling me—really critical surgery. Gotta go!"

He hung up the phone and shoved it under the blanket out of her reach. She menacingly circled the bed.

"What's going on?"

"I have something to tell you," he said. He took a deep breath and collected his thoughts. "You lied."

She opened her mouth, a surge of outrage ready to fire. And then, bafflement. Snapping at bafflement's heels was guilt.

"What do you mean, I lied?"

"You lied about being engaged," Corey said.

She looked down at the floor for an instant.

He had her now. Guilt was a very potent weapon on the battlefield of matrimony.

"He never asked you," Corey continued with confidence. "He said he couldn't until he asked his mom. You told me you were engaged because you thought it would make me back off."

"I figured you were in shock."

"I'm fine, Robyn, and I know that you didn't get engaged that night when we had all the neighbors in Aunt Rose's shop. He just called to tell you that his mother was sick and her nurse had begged him not to disturb the old lady with talk about you because an engagement to you would be too upsetting."

"How do you know all that?"

"Because I've been talking to Bob. I've had three conversations with him. He told me there's no engagement."

"You called Bob in Ireland?"

"He called here. For you. But you were asleep two times."

"Why didn't you wake me up?"

"I...well, I don't know!" he exploded. "The first time I just wanted to hear him out. He was calling because he thought you might be mad because he hadn't told his mom. When I figured out that you weren't really engaged..."

"Pre-engaged."

"All right, when I realized it was just a pre-engaged thing, I figured I had a right to try to win you over."

"So Operation Seduce Bob's Fiancée began."

"Yeah. And it worked."

"Operation Seduce Bob's Fiancée," she said, pursing her lips together in a particularly disdainful way. "A successful mission."

Great! he thought, mentally smacking himself on the forehead. He had put the focus back on his wrongdoing. Losing the offensive, a military strat-egist would call it.

Blowing it, that's what us civilians call it, Corey thought, simmering, as she yanked her flannel nightshirt up over her head, giving him what he knew might very well be the final tantalizing look at her naked body silhouetted by the moonlight.

She turned on the nightstand lamp.

They both looked guiltily at Bob's picture, turned down on the nightstand.

"Did you tell him that we…we made love?" Robyn asked.

"No, I didn't even tell him who I am. He thinks I'm my father."

"And what about the part where you said you would tell me gently? What are you supposed to tell me?"

"He still hasn't told his mother—she got a cold the first day he was back, and every time he starts to talk about you she starts sniffling. He thought you might be upset with him for delaying. I told him I'd talk to you for him.''

"And you told him not to rush telling her because she might have a relapse of the common cold?" Robyn asked, pacing around the bed.

"She might. And it could turn into something much worse."

"Like what?"

"I dunno. But she could get really sick."

"That's hardly a medical judgment."

"Bob seemed to believe me."

"And you did this because...?"

"Because I'd do anything to get you to marry me," Corey said defiantly. "My son needs a father. His own father. That would be me."

"You'd do anything, huh?"

"Anything," he confirmed.

"Including making love to me so that I'd say yes to marriage? And if we were married, you'd be a father to Charlie without having to contend with a stepfather in your life."

"It wasn't as cold-blooded as that."

"Give me the phone."

It was just then that he realized his error. "I made love to you because I wanted you," he said, reaching out for her. She stepped back, and he threw off the sheets. For an instant he thought he saw admiration in those emerald green eyes. But then she must have remembered herself and gave him a withering look. He pulled the sheet up over his abdomen. "And I love you. It wasn't just about Charlie. Or Bob."

"Right. Hand me the phone."

"It was good between us, Robyn. You have to admit that. Very good. It always was. It will always be like that."

"Hand me the phone."

"You can't run away from what's between us."

"Hand me the phone."

He looked down at the blanket. Now wouldn't be the right time to ask her if she wanted to get it herself. He pulled the phone out from under the blanket.

"I'm calling Bob, and I'm going to ask him to forgive me," Robyn said, punching in the phone number. "Darn, it's busy."

"Don't try again."

"And if he forgives me, I'll ask him to marry me. Regardless of what his mother says."

"Now you're acting stubborn."

"And then I'm flying to Ireland to meet her. And to marry him."

The phone rang, surprising them both.

Corey lunged. He snatched the phone. She yanked it back.

"It's going to be Bob and I'm going to explain this whole—"

"Are you really willing to tell him everything?"

A poppy red blush blossomed on her cheeks.

"You liked it. You liked it a lot," Corey said softly.

"You tricked me into liking it."

"That's lame, Robyn, truly lame. No, baby, you'd have to explain that you were a willing partner."

The phone rang a second time.

"Nobody forced you into my arms. You'd have to explain how you didn't call out his name when you climaxed, you called out—"

The phone rang again.

"I'm going to explain everything. And he'll probably tell me to go to hell. Then I'm going to tell you the same thing."

She picked up the receiver.

"Hello, Bob?!"

She listened for a moment and then threw the phone at Corey.

"It's some guy named Rusty. Says he's got an emergency. Make it snappy, because I've got a phone call to make."

And she slammed the door behind her.

Chapter Fourteen

"I'm just givin' ya fair warning," Rusty said. "You've always been decent to me, even when you've told me no picture. You've never grabbed my camera or punched me or ripped up perfectly good film. A gentleman, that's what you are."

"Thanks, Rusty," Corey said, slipping on his pants with one hand and keeping an ear cocked for the slam of the apartment door. It hadn't come. Yet. He suspected she was in the living room and that he didn't have a lot of time. Still, he wanted to be sure about every detail. "Just repeat the whole story once more."

"All right, I took my shots to my editor this afternoon, explainin' how I got good ones of the mayor's wife and of yourself. And that dame— your so-called friend of the family—caught his eye. Said he had a tip he was going to run with the picture of you and the gorgeous redhead to-gether."

"And the tip was…?" Corey prompted, waiting for the revulsion he knew would come on hearing it a second time. He could hear this a million times, and the horror wouldn't ebb.

"The tip is that this gal was your father's house-keeper's daughter and she has your illegitimate child and she's going to marry that Irish rock star. What's his name?"

"She is, or was, pre-engaged to an accountant named Bob."

"You mentioned that the first time I told you about the leader of Bumpus, but I still don't know what pre-engaged means. You either is or you ain't engaged."

"She ain't. I mean, she isn't. But Bob's an accountant."

"I've been told you'd deny Bob is the lead singer and guitarist from the band Bumpus."

"She's engaged to a guy named Bob McNitt."

"I wish one of my kids was in the room so I could ask his last name. Bumpus's spokesman has publicly denied that this friend of yours is marrying him or that he is the father of her child. But the editor faxed my pic of the redhead to Ireland, and the group released a statement saying Bob'd be happy to marry her. So naturally that seems like a confirmation."

"Naturally," Corey said flatly.

"So the editor sent a fact checker to pull a copy

of the kid's birth certificate so I sez to him, I sez it ain't right to—"

Corey felt his stomach turning.

"Okay, Rusty, I've heard enough."

"It's a crying shame they're running this. It's not you that gets hurt—a man never gets hurt by rumors of beautiful women. You know that better than most men. But it's the kid I'm thinkin' of. And that, uh, friend of the family."

"Yeah, they both will get hurt," Corey said.

"Buddy, I'm proud of my profession," Rusty waxed on. "There's dames who open the newspaper Monday morning first thing—looking to see if I got their picture in the society page—and boy, don't they feel good when they do!"

"I'm sure they do, Rusty."

"But this investigatin' and uncoverin' is a black eye on the business. So I'm warnin' you. You might want to have your lawyer call before tomorrow's edition."

"I won't do that," Corey said quietly.

"You'll let it run?"

"I have to. It's the truth. Except the part about the band leader of Bumpus."

Rusty whistled.

"Man, that's rough."

Corey was not a man prone to panic or indecision. He was a problem solver, the kind of guy who took a deep breath and a deeper look at a crisis, and this time he came up with a treasure of a solution.

"Rusty?"

"Yes, sir?"

"Do you think your editor would give you a little something extra in your Friday envelope if you had wedding pictures? Exclusive ones?"

"Yours? Oh, yes sirree, he would! For sure."

"And would he hold off on the story until the wedding?"

"I see where you're going," Rusty said. "I think he would hold the story if I gave him a little advance warning. Do I really get exclusives?"

"There won't even be an Instamatic on the premises."

"No scooping me out with a tip to my rival across town?"

"None."

"Sounds enticing. That shot of the Kennedy kid's wedding made that photographer's reputation."

"It could happen to you."

"But what about that rock singer? You remember. Bob from Bumpus."

"Don't worry about Bob. He can't get married without a permission slip from his mother."

"ARE YOU DONE?" Robyn asked, impatiently tapping her foot against the floor. "I've got a phone call to make."

"Don't," Corey said.

He buttoned his shirt and sat down on the easy chair across from her. He looked so sad, so down and low. She nearly reached out to him, but as her hand was poised midair his eyes met hers.

His face had gone hard and unforgiving. He was going to tell her what to do. He was going to put down the rules. He was going to give one of his commands and expect her to obey him because she had weakened and surrendered to his seductive tactics.

Well, never again.

She picked up the phone.

"Put it down, Robyn," he ordered.

"I have to explain to Bob what I've done," she said, dialing stubbornly.

He lunged over the coffee table, putting the receiver down.

"I said don't. We have to talk. I'm going to explain that phone call from Rusty. And then we're getting married on Saturday."

"I'm not getting married to you," she retorted. "And now that you've done your meddling, I'm probably not getting married to Bob, either. Get your hand off my telephone and get the heck out of my apartment."

"You're going to marry me. Because it's the right thing. For Charlie."

There was something new in his voice, something beyond the arrogant assumption that he would be obeyed, something about the way his voice cracked when he said Charlie. She put the phone down and listened to his explanation, and at the end, she put her head in her hands.

"He's three years old," Corey pointed out gently, having used up most of his indignation as he related Rusty's tale. "He's starting nursery school next fall. This'll be remembered. Every parent of the kids in his class will have read the story in the society page. Teachers will, too. It might not make any difference, maybe they'll be tolerant, maybe they'll be cool, but you don't want to take that chance, do you?"

"But they've got Bob mixed up with that rock musician. As soon as people know that that part of the story isn't true…"

"They'll know what's true and what's not."

"And the editor is definitely going to run the piece?"

"If we don't give them something better. Marrying Bob McNitt would lower the scandal quotient," he said. "But Bob's not the kind of man who would understand what we did tonight—not many men are. And you'll tell him because you're that kind of woman. And you're the kind of woman who can't make love to one man and marry another."

"Thanks for destroying my life tonight."

"I'm sorry if you think the only reason I made love to you was to get you to marry me, and I know sorry probably isn't enough. But I'm all you have left. I'm all Charlie's got left.''

She stood up, tugged her night dress into place.

''You can sleep on the couch,'' she said.

''And if I tell you right now that I love you, you'll think I'm only saying the words so I can sleep in bed with you?''

''That's right.'' She walked down the hall.

''Are you going to marry me?'' Corey shouted.

''Yes, damn it,'' she said, slamming the bedroom door.

Her bedroom was ordinarily quite neat—a small, cozy space that she was careful not to let get run over with knickknacks. But there was a cyclone's worth of mess. His shoes on the floor, hers under the bed. A stocking over the headboard, another on the nightstand. Her dress in a puddle by the rocking chair. His suit jacket draped across the dresser.

And everywhere, pieces of her broken heart.

ROBYN AWOKE with her arms around Corey's suit jacket. Sunlight filtered through the budding oak tree and lace curtains. The smell of buttermilk pancakes, Aunt Rose's favorite breakfast, mingled with the lilacs blooming in the backyard. Robyn reached out to the nightstand for her clock, finding the turned-down picture of Bob instead.

''I am so sorry,'' she said guiltily.

On the floor she noticed the glittering Claddagh

ring that she had lost. Oh, what kind of mess had she gotten herself into!

Throughout the night, she had waited for Bob to call her back. She had called, but his mother said he was out again. She had made clear to Mrs. McNitt that no matter how late he returned from his outing, he could call Chicago. When Robyn finally drifted off to sleep at five o'clock, she held the phone in her hand, ready to pick up before Corey beat her to it.

But now she held his jacket, and the phone lay on the floor, and she was sure she would have woken if it had rung. Eight o'clock. Friday morning. She had two fittings, a meeting downtown with a milliner and the whole afternoon to play with Charlie. And her own wedding to ponder.

"Cow-ee! Cow-ee!"

A smile stole across her face at the sound of Charlie's voice. No matter how bad things were, she still had the most wonderful little boy. She threw off the covers and opened the door to the hall. Charlie rolled a basketball down the hard-wood floor to Corey.

"Cow-ee!"

"It's Daddy," Corey said. "Say Daddy."

"Cow-ee!"

The ball rolled by Robyn's feet.

"Ma!" Charlie cried. He ran to hug her, bouncing up and down in her arms. "I go Marg-ee house and John-John there."

"Did you have a good time?"

He nodded, eyes already darting ahead to the hall. He squirmed away. Robyn stood up and met Corey's gaze.

He hadn't slept, either, Robyn would guess, but he had training in missing out on zees. A little stubble on his jaw, his shirt a tad wrinkled, pale lines at the corners of his eyes—nothing a shave, a change of clothes and a cup of coffee couldn't fix.

Robyn self-consciously stepped back into her room. She tugged on a white terry bathrobe just as Corey stood at the doorway. Somehow he must have sensed that he was not welcome to enter. And good thing, because she had done some thinking about last night.

She pulled her hair into a tight ponytail and faced him squarely.

"We need to set some rules about this marriage," she said, her voice shaky but quickly gaining assuredness. "It's in name only."

"What does that mean?"

"This marriage is for Charlie. Not us. Therefore the first rule is that you will not touch me without my permission. We're not making love. Ever again. And I'm on to your seductive tricks. It won't happen again."

"Okay," he said amiably. "What's the next rule?"

He wasn't arguing. Wasn't protesting. Wasn't

even giving her a megawatt smile that said, "You wanted it just as much as I did." She had prepared, organized, memorized and categorized a passel of reasons why this was the best way, the only way, this marriage was going to work. Working out what to say, she had practiced a concluding paragraph with an admission that she'd seen the wisdom of marrying for Charlie's sake, but it was just that—for Charlie's sake.

She felt oddly deflated by Corey's quick concession to her rule. And the more she thought about it, the more she felt a nudge of anger. Shouldn't he fight her, fight for her, on this one?

"Next rule?"

"I'll think of something," she said.

"While you're thinking, you need to make some choices. Tulips or roses for the wedding?"

"Dead dandelions."

"I'll put you down for tulips," he said, pulling out a slim leather agenda book. "Next, pink champagne or white?"

"Water and bread and thin gruel is standard fare for prisoners."

"Pink champagne," he said, writing in his book. "String quartet or guitar?"

"Anything funereal."

"String quartet. White rice or birdseed?"

"Birdseed. At least something good will come out of this."

"Chocolate wedding cake or vanilla?"

"I won't eat it."

"Chocolate. Honeymoon?"

"No way."

"Okeydokey," he said, picking up Charlie who had come back from the end of the hall. "Come on, Charlie, let's go play while Mommy gets dressed. She's going to have so much to do today."

"I am?" Robyn asked, as the door nearly but not quite shut behind them.

"Yes, I forgot," Corey said. He poked his head into the room. "You have one rule that I have so graciously accepted."

"Uh-oh."

"And I have one rule for this marriage, too."

"You do?"

"Yes. My rule is that you have to pack everything you don't want the movers to touch by eleven o'clock this morning. We're moving today."

And the door shut behind them.

"I DON'T WANT to move," Robyn moaned. "I like my life here just fine."

"I know that, darlin'," Aunt Rose said, putting a plate of pancakes in front of her. "But a man and his wife live together."

"This isn't a real marriage."

"It will be legal and it will have all the essential

elements,'' Corey said. ''Flowers, champagne, wedding cake, bride and groom.''

''You left out love,'' Robyn said.

Rose sat at the head of the table.

''You know, children, I thought that if I took Charlie away for the night you'd get yourselves resolved.''

Charlie squirmed in his booster seat. He had made a series of tunnels and rivers and mountains with his pancakes and syrup.

''I done,'' he announced.

''You're excused, baby,'' Robyn said.

As soon as Charlie was out of the kitchen, Rose leaned forward and confronted the two.

''I want to know what happened last night,'' she said, and sat back to watch Robyn and Corey glare at each other. ''Oh, I get it. You made love.''

Robyn twisted her napkin.

''Aunt Rose, I have a confession to make. Corey made love to me because he wanted me to marry him.''

''Scandalous,'' Aunt Rose said blandly. ''I've never heard of a man acting so callous.''

''And I thought I was cheating on Bob,'' Robyn continued, ignoring her aunt's sarcasm. ''But it's a little more complicated than that.''

''Really?''

''I'm not engaged to him.''

''Good.''

''And now that Corey and I have...''

"Made love," Corey prompted. Robyn shot him a look.

"Bob wouldn't marry me if he knew."

"You can't marry him at all," Corey said. "You have to marry me. Rose, we also have a little newspaper problem. It's my fault for thinking we could go to the party, night before last, and not have someone notice."

Together, in fits and starts, the couple explained the phone call from Rusty and the ensuing proposal. Aunt Rose shook her head, clucked sympathetically and disapprovingly at certain disclosures and took a long drag on her coffee at the end of their tale.

"Living together in holy matrimony is the only way to make Charlie's life right," she concluded. "You'd better make your peace before the wedding so's you don't make everybody miserable. Yourselves included. I could have told you this all last night. I suppose there's only one thing that you've cleared up for me with all your confessin'."

"What's that?" Robyn asked.

"A little teenybopper approached me just as I was coming home with Charlie," Aunt Rose said, rising to her feet. "She asked me if Bob lived here and if he did, would he sign her autograph book because she was the president of the local chapter of his fan club."

"Oh, no," Robyn said. "What's going to happen when Bob comes home?"

"He'll be mighty popular with the seventeen-and-under crowd," Aunt Rose observed. She drained her coffee and left the kitchen.

"Peace?" Corey asked, offering his right hand across the table. "We've got eighteen years ahead of us, and Aunt Rose is absolutely right—we can't let our pride and stubbornness get in the way of Charlie's happiness. You'll follow my rule."

"You follow mine."

He nodded. "We'll manage," he said. He caught her look of doubt. "For Charlie's sake," he amended. "Peace."

"Okay, peace," Robyn said, though as she shook his hand she felt anything but peaceful.

Chapter Fifteen

At eleven o'clock the last two movers put the toy
box in Charlie's new playroom and accepted an
Andrew Jackson each from Corey in addition to
the company overtime charges.

Aunt Rose was already snoring in her second-
floor bedroom on the chiropractor-endorsed mat-
tress. Charlie cuddled his teddy bear in the bedroom adjoining the playroom.

Both were exhausted from their efforts at moving into the Astor Street house. Charlie had spent
hours arranging his action figures in the playroom
built-in cabinets, while Aunt Rose's work largely
centered on telling the movers what to do.

Robyn finished her business assignments at noon
and had changed from her suit into a pair of over-
alls for the long day.

Then she called Ireland and left Corey's phone
number. Bob was out with friends but expected
back shortly. She eyed the phone several times dur-

ing the day, but even her strong will couldn't get it to ring.

She sorted through client files, put up pictures in the playroom and stacked the O'Halleran Sunday-best china in the cabinet right on top of the Harte family Wedgewood plates.

She unloaded her boxes in the converted attic—after refusing Corey's offer to share the master bedroom.

"It's my rule."

"I can sleep in a bed with you and not touch you."

"No way. Nobody knows what goes on behind the doors of this house," she explained. "And that means I sleep in my own bedroom. You sleep in yours."

Then she called Ireland and told Bob's mother again that Bob could call her at any hour.

"You just missed him," Bob's mother said cheerily. "He went back out again. To a soccer match with my nurse."

"Shouldn't your nurse be taking care of you?"

"I'm not an invalid," Mrs. McNitt snapped. "Besides, since Bob is returning to America tomorrow I thought my nurse could do with a little outing. She's older, extremely shy and doesn't get out much. I gave her the day off."

"That's very kind of you. And Bob, too. But I really need to talk to him, so could you tell him to call whenever he gets in—preferably before he gets on the plane home?''

''I surely will. And what did you say your name was again?''

Robyn spelled her name slowly and carefully thinking all the while that Bob must not have told his mother about marrying her yet. Otherwise, Mrs. McNitt wouldn't keep asking her to respell it every time she called.

''Have him call me, please. It's very important, Mrs. McNitt.''

She hoped Bob wouldn't tell his mother before the flight back home. If Robyn could talk to Bob first, explain the events of the past few days, break up with him gently—he wouldn't have to upset his mother at all.

When she heard the movers thanking Corey for their tip, she went downstairs, drawn by the un-mistakable smells of dinner. The dining room table was set for two, votive candles dotted the white organdy cloth, and soft jazz wafted from the speakers discreetly hidden in the walls.

Displayed on one of the elegantly etched plates was a small robin's egg blue box from Tiffany's with a white ribbon tied just so.

Is this how he planned to follow her rule? she wondered.

''Hello, Robyn.''

''Ashford,'' she said, breaking into a smile when

she recognized her deb escort. "It's nice to see you."

He wore a charcoal gray suit, a crisply starched white shirt and a red bow tie. He stepped through the swinging kitchen door and kissed her lightly on the cheek.

"Are you staying for dinner?"

He shook his head. "Corey already asked me but no. I have to pick up Lelaine—you remember her from your coming out and from night before last. I was just the delivery boy for Corey."

"Delivery?"

"Tiffany's. Picked it up this afternoon while you two were working on the move." He kissed her cheek. "See you tomorrow. Corey's made me best man."

"That's nice of you to agree to stand up for him," Robyn said.

Ashford regarded her carefully. "Try not to look so somber. It's not like you're being thrown into a pond with starving crocodiles. Brides are supposed to blush and smile. It gives the rest of us hope. And do me a favor—aim the bouquet at Lelaine. She won't say yes to me and she won't say no. Torture. Pure torture."

"But you love her."

A sweetly boyish smile stole over his face. "Oh, yeah, I do. I really do love her. And she'll never know it wasn't me who switched place cards at the ball."

"Your secret's safe."

After saying goodbye, Robyn picked up the Tiffany's box and slipped off the white satin ribbon.

"It's an engagement ring," Corey said, coming in with a glass of white wine. "Could you wear it with my mother's ring?"

He pulled the ring from his pocket—the one she had worn for four years. She took it, put it on her left finger and then opened the box. Inside was a large pear-shaped diamond set on a gold band.

"Ashford dropped it off for me," he said, adding ruefully, "It's four years late, isn't it? Does it fit?"

She slipped it on so that it lay flush against Robyn's mother's ring.

"Tomorrow I'll put another band on your hand. One that matches my mother's," he said. "This one's five carats."

"I see," Robyn said, tentatively pulling at the ring. It didn't budge. "I don't need a ring."

"Yes, you do. You're going to be a married woman. My married woman," he said. "Robyn, why are you taking it off?"

"I'd take it off if I could but it's stuck!"

"Don't panic. Just stop pacing. Here, relax and twist the ring slightly."

"I did that."

"So leave it on. Most women are happy to have a diamond ring on their finger."

"Most women get their diamonds from men

who love them.'' She silenced his protest with an upheld hand. "I thought we had an agreement. I followed your rule—I'm moved in. And you're not following mine.''

He stepped back, holding up his hands.

"I haven't touched you.''

"You don't eat like this every night. Music, candlelight, fine china....''

"No, but...''

"And you don't hand out diamonds like this every day.''

"No, but...''

No buts! She was already halfway up the back staircase, tugging and twisting and tugging some more.

"Robyn, come back. At least let me help you get it off.''

"No.''

"I'm a doctor,'' he yelled up the stairs. "I'll put some ice on it. If you keep working it you'll make your finger swell up and then you'll have to have the ring cut off.''

"That's not a bad suggestion,'' she said.

"Does this mean you're not having dinner with me?''

"This means good night,'' she said, closing the bedroom door.

SHE PUT VASELINE on the ring, but the only thing it did was make for a greasy ring. She put her hand under the faucet, but cold water made her shiver. She wrinkled her nose at the sparkling diamond, thinking if she were only a witch she could make it disappear.

Five carats.

Five big, strapping carats.

With a romantic dinner and mood music, a diamond ring to seal the deal, he had hoped to bring her into his bed.

And under his thumb.

He should have just bought handcuffs while he was at it.

Trophy wife.

That's what she must be to him—the part of the job description that he had forgotten to mention when they had been talking about Charlie's well-being.

Robyn was going to be a trophy wife to show off the wealth and prestige of young Dr. Harte. With just a wave of her hand.

She knew many other women wouldn't mind trading positions. She knew many other women would like a father in the picture, a diamond on their hand, a spacious house and financial security.

Four years she had paid her own bills, made her own decisions, did what was necessary to not just survive but to thrive. She was proud of herself— not so much that she could ever brag, but enough that she could look herself in the mirror and say that she was doing her best. She was a successful businesswoman and a responsible and loving mother and niece.

She wasn't to be displayed as a prize he won, and she wouldn't give up her principles for a glittering rock on her hand.

It's a beautiful ring, a voice inside her head said. *You're crazy for not wanting to wear it.*

"I'd want to wear it if it was a symbol of love," Robyn said. "And this isn't love, this is pride. His pride."

She heard a rustling at the door.

"Hi," he said, handing her a bowl of ice. "I brought this up. It might help get the ring off."

"Thank you," she said stiffly, and then as he turned to go, "Rule number three—no trying to seduce me."

"Robyn, I can't help it if you find me attractive over a nice meal."

"One last rule," she said. "Don't buy me things. No more diamonds. I'm able to provide for myself, and it's a point of pride that I do. You can buy things for Charlie. And for Aunt Rose. But not for me."

"Fine," he said wearily.

"So we're clear. No touching. No romancing. No gifts."

"Sure."

"Thank you for the ice," she said. "When I get the ring off I'll give it back to you. I'll just wear a simple wedding band because every married woman does. But that's it.''

"Fine," he said curtly.

She shut the door and shoved her hand in the bowl of ice. It was punishingly cold—just the thing she needed after that confrontation.

She sat for ten minutes before trying to twist the ring off again. It didn't work. She put the ice in the bathroom sink and lay down on the length of the bed.

But she couldn't sleep.

She kept remembering...

The times he played tea party with her dolls, treating her six-year-old self as he would an experienced and enchanting hostess—what thirteen-year-old boy would have the patience...or the charm?

And then the third-grade class bully who sent her home bruised and crying—Robyn had no idea what Corey said or did, but she was never hassled again.

The years she spent at boarding school—what a crush she had had. And hadn't her lack of experience been directly attributable to her comparing every boy to Corey, and every boy came up short? It was that lack of experience that had been her undoing at the debutante ball....

How was she ever going to live in peace with him?

She crept downstairs to the second-floor bedroom. With a sliver of the hall light to guide her, she lay on the twin bed next to Charlie. He stirred, finding her by instinct, and flopped his arm on her stomach.

Although she would have tossed and turned upstairs in her own bed, Charlie's rhythmic breathing calmed and focused her. If she just kept his well-being as her goal, she would know what to do. She put away all thought, all worry and at long last found sleep.

That was how Corey found her an hour later when he, too, could not find peace. He sat on the edge of the bed and watched them sleep until he memorized their features and reached behind him to turn off the hall light. She lay on her side, one arm cradling Charlie's head.

He was charged with protecting them both, and he would do it with every ounce of his strength. He would provide for both of them—neither would ever want for anything. He knew no other role for himself as a father and a husband.

But why couldn't Robyn accept that from him?

He tried telling her she was marrying him. She wouldn't listen.

Tried making love to her. Didn't make her feel any better about him when she caught on about his conversations with Bob.

Tried a list, even though it wasn't his style. Still didn't work.

Tried candlelight dinners and diamonds. Surefire methods.

Didn't work.

Corey squirmed on the twin bed, looking for a comfortable way to sit. His eyes felt a little dry and heavy, nothing unusual—he was used to no sleep and he knew he had several hours left in him.

He wouldn't even fall asleep if he put his elbow down and propped his head up on his arm. So he did.

He picked up a stuffed teddy bear from the floor. One with a soft, round stomach. He'd lay his head on the teddy—he wasn't that tired. Actually, he was pretty agitated. The ring really made her mad and he would have thought she would have been happy about a five-carat diamond.

Rules! Rules! Rules and more rules! Was married life with Robyn going to be as complicated as the I.R.S. code?

He looked at the offensive piece of carbon that sparkled daintily in the glow of the streetlight.

It was a ring that—admit it, man—was a mite ostentatious. Bigger was better, had been his thinking about diamonds. The salesclerk at Tiffany's had told him that all women liked diamonds, and they liked them better than simple gold bands inherited from Mom. Why would Robyn be so different from the rest of the female population?

And then he remembered how he had asked for

the engraving which took an extra week and how Ashford had to pick up the diamond.

But when Robyn had made clear she didn't want to see him ever again, Corey hadn't the heart to pick up the diamond or even to make arrangements for a return of his money.

He took her hand and checked. Yup! That ring was tight. Good thing her finger wasn't swelling up around the ring. He kissed her finger, remembering how she had so many years ago come to him when she had boo-boos.

The last conscious thought he had was that he'd get her a bowl of ice in the morning, shove her hand in it, take off the ring and buy her a new one.

Robyn O'Halleran would be the first, last and only customer in Tiffany's history to return a diamond ring and ask for a smaller one.

Chapter Sixteen

"He's coming home! He's coming home!"

Aunt Rose pounded on Robyn's door, got no reply, opened the door, found the room empty and raised her eyes heavenward.

"Saints in heaven preserve us! I'd better find that girl in Corey's room. It's the only way we'll avoid disaster!"

She took the back staircase to the second floor and knocked on the master bedroom door.

"He's coming home!"

No answer.

"I said he's coming home!"

She squeezed her eyes shut and tried the door.

"Robyn? Corey? I have the most terrible news," she said, stepping into the room.

She opened one eye. Then the other. The bed, a king-size teakwood four-poster, was empty. Its white-and-blue Lindbergh-patterned quilt was unwrinkled, its white pillowcases crisply starched.

Where were they?

"He's coming home!"

On the second floor, Robyn opened her eyes. She felt Charlie stirring in her arms. A ribbon of sunlight cut across her cheeks.

Aunt Rose was yelling about something, but whatever it was, it couldn't be more important than a few more minutes of sleep.

She turned over and met hard, lean muscle.

Muscle opened his eyes.

Eyes the color of blue skies.

"Happy wedding day," he said softly, breaking the magic spell of sleep.

Robyn sat up. "You broke rule number one," she said. "Your hand was on me."

"I was asleep."

"Still counts. You took advantage of me because I was asleep."

"I was hardly in a position to take advantage of you. I was asleep, too."

"You shouldn't be in my bed."

"This isn't your bed."

"Still…"

"It's Charlie's bed," he interrupted. "Neutral territory."

"He's coming home!"

Aunt Rose lumbered into the bedroom, breathing hard as she collapsed on the rocker.

"Who's coming home?"

"Bob. His mother called this morning and said

that Bob is returning to America,'' Rose panted. ''His flight gets into O'Hare airport at twelve-thirty.''

''Oh, my God,'' Robyn said.

''And she said he's coming to get married!''

''Oh, no,'' Robyn moaned, rubbing her temples with her fingers. ''He must have told her. That poor man, that poor man. He's been so good to me, always been by my side, so supportive and now...''

''Don't start that,'' Corey ordered, rising to his feet. ''You're marrying me. At one o'clock.''

''But he'll be expecting me to meet him at the airport!''

''I'll send a limo for him.''

Robyn shook her head.

Bob was so good. He didn't deserve to come home to this. Didn't deserve any of this. It was all her fault, and the least she owed him was to meet him at the airport and explain everything.

''Get him out of your head,'' Corey growled. ''It's our wedding day. And it's already nine-thirty. We've just got three and a half hours before we're joined in wedding bliss.''

''You broke my rule last night,'' Robyn reminded him.

''I'll put a lock on your bedroom door.''

''I won't be a prisoner.''

''You'll be the only one with a key.''

''And as soon as I get this ring off...''

He was already down the hall. "I'm taking a shower," he said. "The caterer and the florist will be here in half an hour."

Robyn looked at Aunt Rose for support. "It was good for you to sleep next to a man," Aunt Rose observed. She tsked softly as Robyn reared her head back. "It gave you a nice healthy glow," she added. "Just the sort of thing a bride needs."

"Please don't play matchmaker," Robyn said gently. "This is a marriage for one purpose only. For Charlie's well-being."

"Sure it is," Aunt Rose said, rocking contentedly.

PRESTON TRUE should have been having a good morning.

He was catering the wedding of the year, even if it was entirely too small and casual for his tastes.

He had purchased a new Sulka paisley silk shirt for the occasion, on the off chance any photographer from the *Tribune* was around when the reporter asked him for details about the wedding.

He had called every friend he knew—and even a few business competitors—to share the news that the lead guitarist from Bumpus was returning from the Ireland concert to marry a beautiful redhead.

And, Preston always added in a confidential tone, he's allergic to fish and berries.

"It so limits the menu," he would sigh to awestruck audiences.

The fact that Bumpus's spokesman denied the wedding would take place only added to Preston's prestige. After all, everybody knows that whatever a spokesman denies must be true and whatever a spokesman declares true must be false.

Preston True had had a good morning while he was dressing, while he was moussing his hair, while he was chatting on the phone with a potential client and breezily announced he had to ta-ta because he was doing the Bumpus wedding.

Preston True had a good morning in the kitchens of Entre Vous, even teasing the assistant pastry chef about the names Bob and Corey and Robyn iced into the top layer of the cake.

Preston nearly, but not quite, sliced off Corey's name with an icing knife—then decided it would jinx things if he did.

Preston True was even having a good morning standing in the chaos of the kitchen of Corey's Astor Street residence. Smoke billowed from the oven. A large blob of pastry dough was stuck to the ceiling. The assistant chef was screaming French invectives at the pastry chef who smacked a rolling pin against his palm as he muttered dangerously. The pert little waitress who took too many acting classes to be useful was applying full makeup, using a soup cauldron for a mirror. Three assistants straight from the Art Institute methodically arranged blanched vegetables on a tray—at the rate they were going, crudités would be passed out as midnight snacks.

And the bride kept asking for bowls of ice to be delivered to her room. If she didn't stop soon, there wouldn't be enough to chill the champagne to the perfect temperature—two degrees below zero.

Preston True did, after all, have very exacting standards. That's why he was a celebrity caterer.

The problems he faced this morning were minor. The necessary unexpecteds were to be expected in any event of any note.

The kitchen telephone rang, and the bartender, taking a break from slicing lemons and limes and his fingers, announced it was a reporter from the *Tribune* asking for Preston.

Impressed, his staff watched as Preston tugged the cuffs of his new shirt and took the phone.

"You's Preston True?" a gravelly voice asked.

"Yes, I am Preston," Preston said, rising to his full height. "Would you like me to spell my name for you?"

"Won't be necessary. You talked to my editor?"

"Yes, I did."

"Told him everything about the Bob wedding, didja?"

"Everything. Everything."

"We need another interview."

"I can talk on the phone," he said, anxiously eyeing his staff.

"And a picture."

"Oh," Preston said. Smiling. "I see."

"Meet me out back in the alley."

"In the alley? But the sun is facing the alley and if you take my picture there, my cheeks will be overexposed. I think the park across the street has much better lighting."

"Jes shaddup and meet me in the alley."

Preston sputtered a reply to a dial tone. Then he hung up, took a comb out of his pocket, touched up his 'do, and slapped his cheeks for color.

He uttered four staccato sentences in French at the assistants working on the crudités, took the rolling pin from the pastry chef and shoved it in a drawer beneath the sink and soothed the aspiring actress-slash-waitress with an affectionate pat on the back.

As he strode out the back door, Preston True thought he was having a very good morning indeed.

And he was.

Right up to the moment he shook hands with the short, squat gentleman in a houndstooth jacket who waited for him in the alley with a camera and a truly spectacular right hook that clipped Preston True's nose, making him bleed all over the paisley Sulka shirt.

UPSTAIRS, Robyn crawled under Charlie's bed to talk to her son. "You just have to wear this for a few hours,'' she said.

"No like," Charlie said. He slid on his stomach up and down the length of the bed.

If Robyn could have caught him she would have dragged him right out into the open.

"I know you don't like it. I wouldn't have picked it out myself. But your dad did his best."

"Cow-ee."

"That's right. Cow-ee. You can call him Daddy."

"Cow-ee."

"All right. Call him anything you want, but get out from under the bed."

Corey, choosing from a catalog of a children's speciality store that promised FedEx delivery, had scored a zero with the ring bearer's outfit.

To be sure, it was finely made. A velvet jumper with a white piqué cotton shirt and a red satin bow tie. Corey had even remembered socks and shoes, so Charlie wouldn't be walking down the aisle in his Velcroed sneakers.

The entire ensemble no doubt looked quite dapper on the catalog model, but Robyn was pretty sure she'd never have a chance to see it in all its splendor on her son. She tried to squeeze out from under the bed, but a curl of her hair got stuck on the bottom coil of the box spring. Charlie scooted out from under the bed.

Now that he had done what she wanted, she needed him back under the bed to help her get out.

"Charlie, get back here!"

She tugged at her hair, yanked hard and freed herself. When she came out from under the bed she was greeted by Lelaine Paik and Ashford, who had blocked Charlie's path out the bedroom door. Ashford wore a dark suit while Lelaine wore a pale peach coat dress and matching pumps. Lelaine kissed Robyn's cheeks and offered her congratulations.

"It's Corey who deserves the congratulations, darling," Ashford said. "For winning her hand—and her heart." He put Charlie up on his shoulders. "Is the little guy giving you some trouble?"

"Trouble dressing," Robyn admitted. She stood up and shook off the dust that clung to the front of her jeans. "It's only an hour before the wedding, and I can't get him in his suit."

"I'll take care of that," Ashford said. "How 'bout giving me a hand, Lelaine?"

"Good luck," Robyn said. She gave him the tie, the jumper and the socks. "The shoes are in the box over there on the floor."

Ashford eyed the desk.

"What's the bowl of ice for?"

"Getting this ring off."

"You don't like it?"

"No. I don't. It's too...big."

"Would you have liked it four years ago?" Ashford asked.

"What kind of question is—"

"No, really, think about the question. Would the Robyn O'Halleran who went to the debutante ball have liked that ring the next morning?"

Robyn looked at the ring. Thought about the kind of girl she had been.

"Yes, if Corey had given it to me, I would have been thrilled by it."

"Then that's all that matters," Ashford said, putting Charlie down on the floor. "Now get out of here. We have a boy to dress. Charlie, please, don't do that. Get out from under the bed."

From under the bed came raucous giggling.

"See, darling, we could have one of these," Ashford said to Lelaine.

"You mean the bed or the child?" she teased.

"The child—although I'd want to get a license to make it legal."

"Get on upstairs," Lelaine told Robyn, ignoring Ashford's obvious reference to marriage. "If you don't go now, you'll never get dressed in time. Do you want your ice?"

"No, it's hopeless," Robyn said. "I'll never get the ring off."

"I thought that was the whole point of marriage," Lelaine said.

"THIS IS TOO MUCH, Corey. You're not supposed to be in here, much less..."

On the bed, propped up against a row of pillows as comfortably as a pasha, was Corey. He wore his black tuxedo, a white starched shirt and white damask vest. His white silk tie was undone, and his black formal shoes were untied.

He looked like a bed-ready Cary Grant, and Robyn didn't like the feelings he provoked in her. Lust. Desire. Wanting.

"Close the door, Robyn," he said. "I've come to a decision."

"Oh, really?" she said, recovering quickly. "Give me the key to my room and we'll talk. Outside. I don't want you in my bed. It's too dangerous."

"Actually, I'll just say what I have to say and then I'll leave."

She crossed her arms over her chest. "I'm listening," she said.

"I've decided to give you your freedom."

On Aer Lingus flight 467 to Chicago, the senior flight attendant checked her passenger list and showed it to her partner.

"It's not the same last name," she said.

"He would never travel under his own name."

"Doesn't look anything like him," the senior flight attendant said, hazarding another glance at the passenger in 4B.

"All celebrities are like that," her colleague

said. "They travel extra grungy looking. So nobody'll recognize them."

"Why would he fly coach class?"

"Even more incognito."

"I'm going to ask for his autograph."

"He won't give it to you. I hear he's awful about that."

"Then why be a rock star if you don't want people to recognize you and fuss over you and want your autograph? It doesn't make any sense to work all that time to be famous and then not do anything about it."

Her colleague shrugged.

The flight attendant walked down the aisle and leaned close to the passenger in 4B. He was perfectly ordinary. Stocky, shorter and older than she expected, but with strawberry blond hair, a nice smile and black-framed glasses that didn't hide his pale green eyes.

"How are you enjoying your flight, sir?"

"Just fine, thank you, miss."

"The pilot told me to relay to you the message that there will be a limousine waiting for you at the downstairs concourse. Near where the cabs are."

"Really?"

"Yes. The driver will hold up a sign with your name. Just your first name. So you don't need to worry about being recognized. And one other thing?"

"Yes?"

The flight attendant took a deep breath.

"Could I have your autograph?" she asked. Her next words were unrehearsed and therefore not as well organized as she would have liked. "I've listened to your music since I was in eighth grade. I always thought you were cuter than the drummer. I bought every album you've ever done. And when you used to sing 'Love Me All Night, Baby' it gave me goose bumps. I asked the band to play that three times at my high school prom. If I could just have your autograph I'd be the happiest woman in all America. Ireland, too."

The woman seated in 4A leaned forward and stared at the flight attendant.

"I beg your pardon," the passenger in 4B said coldly, "but I'm an accountant."

The flight attendant, with a red-hot blush on her face, straightened up and wiped away the wrinkles on her skirt.

"Certainly, Bob. Can I call you Bob? It's okay. I understand. You don't want to be noticed," she said, making a zipping motion across her lips. "I'll never tell a soul your real identity. Take that glass for you?"

Bob McNitt gave her his glass, thinking it was odd that she would so carefully fold his napkin and put it the pocket of her uniform.

Then the senior flight attendant headed for the first-class galley where she confided in the four other flight attendants on duty that the passenger in 4B was definitely, thrillingly, no doubt about it—Bumpus's lead guitarist and singer and she had his lip imprint on a napkin to keep forever.

Chapter Seventeen

"You're giving me my freedom?" Robyn asked, closing the door.

"Yes, Robyn," Corey confirmed. "I'm setting you free."

"What about Charlie and the newspaper story?"

"I'll square it with the publisher."

"How?"

"Money does things. That's what it's for. A little will go a long way in this situation—especially if I couple it with a threat of litigation."

Robyn stood stiffly at the side of the dresser. "And how about raising him?"

"We'll do it any way you want. I'd like to be there, involved every step of the way. If I can't live with you, I'll live near you—whether you choose to be on Astor Street, in Little Village or even on the top of Mount Everest."

"And marriage?"

"That's a funny thing," he said, putting his

hands behind his head. "Marriage is love and love is marriage. As Frank Sinatra said, they go together like a horse and carriage."

"And?"

"And I'm thinking marriage comes with only one rule—the rule to love and honor, cherish and protect until death do us part."

He stood up, ducking his head to avoid the sloping ceiling. When he pulled himself up to his full height, he missed the peak of the ceiling by an inch and he dominated the room.

He took two steps toward her and traced a line from her cheek to her collarbone…and then ruefully pulled his hand back.

"I love Charlie," he said. "I am his father and I admit that life would be easier on all of us if I could marry you. But I won't marry you this way."

"You won't?"

"No. Marriage isn't about rules for no touching and separate bedrooms and fighting over whether you'll live with me. It's about love, which—I know, I know, you think I'd just be saying I love you because I want to marry Charlie's mom—"

"Well, you would be."

"No, Robyn, you don't get it. I want what I had last night, if ever so briefly. The right to lie down next to you. That's what marriage is. What it should be. I thought it didn't matter, that I could play however you set up the game," he said. "But when I slept next to you last night, I realized I want that every night. And if we can't have it together, I don't think we have any business marrying.''

Robyn swallowed hard. ''Does that mean you're sending the guests home?''

''It means I'm going down there, and I'll wait for you. Give this some thought. If you don't come walking down the aisle, I'll respect your decision,'' he promised. ''I won't like it, but I'll respect it. If you marry Bob, that's your choice, and we've got a judge, flowers, champagne, and Bob'll like the price. It'll be on me. Or you can say you don't want to marry either of us.''

''And if I come down the aisle to you?'' she asked in a very small voice.

''I'll expect all the rights and privileges of a husband,'' he explained.

''All of them?''

''Including the right to touch you here,'' he said, cupping her breasts with his hands.

''Oh, Corey…''

''And here.'' He pushed apart her legs with his knee and pressed against her hips. ''And here.''

He brought his head down and kissed her. With an initial hesitancy that let her think, just for a moment, that she was still in charge, still setting the pace, still making the rules.

And then masculine instinct took over. His mouth widened, demanding her lips follow his and he plunged his tongue into her mouth, exploring and tantalizing her softest flesh.

And he showed her just what marriage would mean.

When fireworks had gone off in her head...

When her knees had weakened so that she relied for balance on his leg thrust between hers...

When her hands tugged at his shirt to bring him closer...

When she had been almost completely—not quite thoroughly, within an inch of her life—been kissed...

Then and only then he let go of her.

He steadied her with his hand on her shoulder, but offered not a smidgen more of that sweet kiss or his powerful caress.

"I loved you then and I love you now," he said hoarsely. "You can believe me or not. Your choice. But if you walk down those stairs and marry me, you'll be in my bed tonight. And every night for the rest of our lives."

He picked up her hand and studied the ring.

"It's a big diamond. Flashy, I know. But it's a young man's ring. I thought it would impress you, thought it would remind you of me even when I couldn't give you what you needed. Something more than my mother's ring."

She pulled her hand back.

"If you want to leave it on, we're getting married. My way. The old-fashioned way."

"Why are you doing this?"

"Because I have to set you free or you'll never

believe me when I say I love you," he said. "And I do love you."

"Then why didn't you—"

"I'm walking down those stairs, Robyn, and it'll only be the second time in my life that I haven't known what's going to happen next. When I haven't controlled the outcome, when I haven't had my way."

"What was the first?"

But he had already strode out the door without a backward glance. The door slammed behind him.

Robyn felt as if the wind had been knocked out of her.

The second time he hadn't been in control?

Heck, she had only just now grown into control of her life, only in the past few months. And then he had come back into her life.

Still, she had managed to stay in control, sure of herself, determined to put this arrangement into its own little compartment.

Except, of course, for some slipups which were the product of her weakness for him.

But that's why she had rules.

Rules and rules and more rules.

Now she had none of the protection of a rule book.

"In his bed? Every night? Rest of our lives?"

But does he love me? she wondered.

"He's finally come to his senses," she said, twisting her ring. "I should focus on the fact that he understands that marriage is not necessary in this situation.''

She slid the ring up to the knuckle—this was always where the trouble began. She waited for the inevitably unyielding swell of flesh, a certain shade of purple at the tips and then she'd grimace and give up.

But something different happened this time— maybe it was the Vaseline, the ice, the cup of coffee she'd had this morning, the lower air pressure or the higher air pressure or maybe just that the ring got tired of being where it wasn't wanted.

The flesh gave way, the ring popped over the knuckle, and Robyn, who had been pulling and tugging for nearly twelve hours without success, was so startled she momentarily let go of it—and the ring went sailing across the room and *clinked* as it hit the floor.

Gone was the sparkle and dance of light, gone was the rainbow that shimmered on her finger.

She got on her hands and knees and found nothing on the floor but dustballs and two paper clips.

The nerve of that man!

In his bed every night!

Rest of our lives!

She would so like to go downstairs right now and tell him to shove off. To forget it. She was a devoted mother and a hardworking business-woman. She wasn't his slave who would obey his every command. He couldn't tell her that she was to be in his bed every night. He couldn't touch her like that. He couldn't lay down the law.

But he could.

She knew it, even if she didn't like it.

It was his kisses that doomed her. His kisses. His touch. His lovemaking.

"I love him," she said miserably. "Damn it, I *love* him."

And, however much she might hate herself, she would do everything he said. Because she loved him.

Everything she had done in the past four years—all the hard work, responsibility, taking charge of matters, making decisions for herself, it was all gone now. She was in his sway and would remain there forever. Because she loved him.

It was at that moment, putting her head down on the cool floor and thinking that love was a terribly cruel joke on her, that she noticed the tiny glint of light. It wasn't the brash, oversize diamond that caught her eye. Oh, no, it was the setting it was in.

She picked it up, squinted, held it up to the light, and decided she needed a magnifying glass.

"Aunt Rose?" she called out. "Where's your sewing basket?"

"OKAY, I GIVE UP. Where's the blushing bride?" Ashford asked.

Charlie and the two men stood in the butler's

pantry just off the living room. Ashford pushed the swinging door just a little to look at the guests.

"Corey, answer me, buddy. They're getting restless out there."

"She's upstairs," Corey said impatiently. "Ashford, that red thing's supposed to be a tie."

Ashford looked down at Charlie, who was driving a plastic tank up his pant leg.

"I thought it was a cummerbund."

"And don't you think he should wear something on his feet?"

"It's a casual, low-key wedding," Ashford protested. "Besides, I had enough trouble getting the velvet jumper on him. Wrestling with your boy is like trying to stuff fifty snakes into a peanut butter jar."

Judge Campbell poked his head into the pantry.

"Gentlemen, we need to start," he said. "I have court time at the tennis club at three and it's already two."

Corey glanced up the stairwell that ran all the way up the house.

He didn't hear a sound.

"Want me to get her?" Ashford asked.

"No, just tell the string quartet to get started and to play extra loud," Corey said, adjusting his tie. "If she hears it, she'll come. If she's gonna come. If she wants to come."

He picked up Charlie, walked out into the living room, accepted the premature congratulations of his guests with as much good grace as he could manage, and it was then that he noticed the crowd on the sidewalk across the street.

He leaned over the large-brimmed hat of one of Aunt Rose's bridge partners, straining to read the hand-painted banner that stretched the length of the curb.

LOVE ME ALL NIGHT, BABY!!!

"Hey, isn't that the name of the Bumpus album that went platinum?" Ashford asked at his shoulder. "Here, let me take the big guy."

"Want Cow-ee," Charlie said, and he made a healthy grab for Corey's ear.

"You're supposed to be the ring bearer," Ashford said, tugging hard. "I've been very patient with you, but I've reached my limit. Take the pillow and let's go up the aisle like a good boy."

"Da-a-ddy!"

"All right, all right," Ashford said. "I'll take the pillow."

ROBYN SAT on Aunt Rose's bed with the contents of the sewing basket spread out in front of her. She held a delicately filigreed magnifying glass in one hand and her engagement ring in the other.

Four years. The ring was four years old—the engraved date on the inside of the band was the day after the debutante ball.

It was still a big diamond. Still brash and show-offy. It was a young man's diamond. Proud and a touch demanding.

"No, it's just right," she said.

And now she knew when the first time in his life had been when he hadn't known what would happen. It was when he'd got on a plane for New York and had hoped that she would be there for him four years later.

She heard Charlie's voice calling Daddy.

Tears started to roll down her face.

She put away the contents of the sewing basket, put the diamond ring on her finger and ran up the back staircase to the third-floor bedroom.

She dressed quickly, tugging the white dress over her shoulders even as she hopped on one foot to wiggle out of her jeans. She assumed the commotion outside was wedding guests, but they seemed awfully loud. She cranked open the window and looked through the filtering screen of oak leaves.

"Oh, no," she said.

She ran downstairs just as the big black stretch limousine pulled up to the house. A thunderous cheer arose from the crowd.

"PLAY IT AGAIN," Corey ordered. "Louder this time. She can't hear it with all that noise outside."

Ashford, standing at his side, nodded at the leader of the quartet at the bay window. The bridal march began again.

"Corey, she's not coming."

"She'll come."

"How do you know?"

"I don't," Corey admitted. "But I guess I've never had any experience at not knowing, at not being in control. If I admit she's not coming, then I'll know I've blown it, Ashford. Really and truly blown it. I'm not sure I'm ready for that."

Judge Campbell leaned close. "Is the bride…here?"

"Let's just wait till the end of the song," Ashford said impatiently. "Then I'll tell the guests that we're not having a wedding."

Corey looked at him.

"It's what a best man is for," Ashford explained.

The quartet repeated the last bars of the bridal march before putting their instruments on their laps. Aunt Rose came out from the kitchen, tugging off her apron. She looked around anxiously. An old man seated in the back of the room coughed.

"Should I start talking?" Ashford asked.

Corey looked down at the ground and sighed. "All right," he conceded. And then he heard it. One step, two and then pitter-patter, faster and faster down the front staircase. He righted his cuffs. "Forget it, Ashford, I'm getting married."

ROBYN KNEW her hair was a tangled, curled, wild mess—she couldn't find her brush, much less the delicately textured veil that Rose had stitched that very morning.

Robyn knew that barefoot brides were more of a hippie fashion, not suitable for an Astor Street wedding—but the box containing the white berib-boned *peau de soie* slippers was nowhere to be found.

She knew brides carried flowers, sometimes a prayer book, but the flowers weren't waiting in the refrigerator and her prayer book was upstairs and she didn't have time to stop for either.

When Charlie tugged out of Corey's arms and ran down the row of seats to her, she was glad she had empty arms to catch him.

All she had was a white dress, a ring and a baby—but then again, that's all she had ever needed to get married to Corey.

She stood at the bottom step, looked out at the faces of her stupefied guests and then tugged her dress into place. She put one naked foot on the floor, silently counted a beat and then put the other one down. Counted and stepped, counted and stepped, with all the grace of a princess bride. The violinist caught on first, the viola rushed through three bars to catch up, and, after consultation with the bassist, the cellist pulled out his bow.

She and Charlie were halfway down the aisle, her eyes had just met Corey's and seen his relief

mixed with awe, forgiveness melted into love—
when the front door burst open.

A pale-haired man in a brown Polo shirt and
khakis stumbled, fell, righted his glasses, tugged a
woman in on top of him and then, rising to his
feet, shoved hard to close the door. Against a horde
of teenage girls who screamed his name and
begged for him to touch them, autograph something, look their way, blow them a kiss, *love them
all night!*

It was only with the extra help of the uniformed
police officer who waded through the crowd and
into the house that he was successful.

As the door slammed, the house became still.

Absolutely still.

"Bob?" Robyn asked. "Are you all right?"

Bob stood up, took the arm of the woman who
accompanied him and pulled her to her feet. At
seeing the undisguised curiosity of the wedding
guests and, perhaps more important, overcome by
the attention which had come her way on coming
to America, the woman tugged at her oatmeal-
colored tweed suit. And cowered behind Bob while
urging him forward.

"Bob, I'm so sorry," Robyn said. "So terribly,
terribly sorry."

Bob looked at Robyn, grimaced and swallowed,
Adam's apple jogging furiously. The officer un-
folded a slip of paper he pulled out of his shirt
pocket.

"I'm looking for a Robyn O'Halleran," he said.

"That's me."

The officer smoothly unclipped his handcuffs from his belt.

"I have a warrant out for your arrest on charges of bigamy," he said.

A ripple of horror swept through the guests. A woman from Aunt Rose's bridge group said she was going to faint, but was revived by her husband fanning a magazine over her face.

The officer scanned the room, his gaze landing with the precision of an eagle on the guilty bride.

"Robyn O'Halleran, you have two outstanding marriage licenses which you obtained from the clerk's office on Tuesday and Wednesday of this week."

Robyn gasped.

"I'm sorry!" she said. "I didn't mean to."

"You can tell that to the judge, miss."

"I can explain this," Walter Greenough said, raising his hand at the back of the room. "It's a simple error in paperwork."

"I still gotta take her in," the officer said, pulling off his aviator frames. "Ma'am, would you relinquish the child and step this way?"

"Over my dead body," Corey declared. "She's marrying me. Right now."

The officer pointed at Robyn and Charlie. "Is that the suspect?"

"Yes, that's her," Judge Campbell said impatiently. "Officer, do you recognize me?"

"Of course, Your Honor," the officer said. He smartly pulled back his shoulders. "I'm in traffic court all the time testifying against moving violations."

"Hand me that warrant."

"Certainly, Judge. It was signed by Judge Talbot."

Judge Campbell opened the warrant. Harrumphed. Hmmed. I see-ed. And then ripped the warrant in two and slipped the pieces into his robe.

"Judge Talbot is such a prissy little weasel," he said. "Doesn't understand the first thing about real life. I'll be meeting with him at three o'clock and we'll resolve the warrant then. Miss O'Halleran, just step right up here please. Officer, could you stand right there until I'm ready for you?"

"Certainly, Your Honor," the officer said, crossing his arms over his chest and surveying the guests for possible lawbreakers.

The violinist picked up his bow, but a stern look from the judge made him reconsider.

Robyn looked back at Bob. The woman behind him peered over his shoulder.

"Bob, I'm getting married," Robyn said.

"I know," he said.

"I'm sorry how it all turned out. I wish I had had a chance to explain. Before you came home."

"Uh, Robyn, I got some explaining to do, too,"

he said, and cleared his throat. "And I wanted—" he looked again at Corey "—I wanted to wish you all the happiness in the world."

"You do?" Corey asked.

Robyn wiped away a tear.

"You deserve every happiness," Bob continued, his voice becoming more steady as his confidence grew. "You are a wonderful woman, and Charlie is a wonderful boy. I love you both very much. But I know that this man—" he held a shaky hand out in Corey's direction "—this man, whom I presume to be Charlie's father, will be a better father to Charlie than I can ever hope to be. Simply because he is…Charlie's father. And Robyn, I know you will be happy with him because your love for him was always, always first in your heart. As much as you always tried to change that, you couldn't change."

It was the longest speech Bob had ever given in any circumstance, including the yearly talk he gave at the Rotary Council reminding members to turn in financial information to their accountants early in the year before the April rush.

The attention, the openmouthed stares of the guests on folding chairs, took a lot out of Bob, but oddly, his talk energized him. When the woman who stood at his side jogged his elbow, he drew up his chin and continued.

"I also came here today to introduce my fiancée," he said, drawing the woman out to his side.

"Sarah is my mother's nurse. And when I went to Ireland, I lost my heart to her. I didn't mean to, Robyn, we never mean to. But we fall in love, don't we? And it's wonderful."

He put his arms around Sarah and beamed.

Sarah ducked her head and waved, then self-consciously put her arms around her fiancé.

Robyn thought Bob had never looked happier.

Judge Campbell cleared his throat. "Can we get this thing moving?" he urged. "I have to be at the tennis court at three o'clock."

Aunt Rose clucked at Bob and told him to bring his fiancée and sit next to her. She took Charlie, and there was a quick exchange of introductions before Aunt Rose, Sarah and Bob sat down with Charlie perched on Bob's lap.

Robyn looked at Corey. "No rules, huh?"

"No rules." He grinned. "Just love, baby, just love."

Judge Campbell sped through the requirements of the wedding vows in record time.

"You may kiss the bride," he said, adding in a whisper. "Make it snappy, Corey. I don't like it when Judge Talbot gets more warm-up time than I do. He's got a killer serve."

Corey had everything he wanted—everything he hadn't known he had wanted until Wednesday. His son. His wife. And a certain Bob McNitt tucked away in a corner of his life called "friend of the family."

It was tough not to feel a certain triumph, an I'm-in-command arrogance.

But one look at Mrs. Robyn O'Halleran Harte changed all that.

She wasn't a little girl anymore. Corey couldn't boss her around, couldn't lord the seven-year age difference over her, couldn't trot out his educational advantages, couldn't change her mind with a stern glance.

She was a woman—she needed and deserved his protection. And she craved and desired all that made him a man. And he was a proud, confident man—but just a man. Just a husband. He glanced at his Charlie who worried his little fist into a thumb's-up—just a father.

A daddy who had gone down the aisle for his son. And for his woman.

He leaned down to kiss Robyn and, no longer his contrarian, she stepped up on her toes to meet him. He swept her up in his arms and knew the glory of having the woman he loved be his. Truly his.

They kissed, and he tasted every sweetness that was her.

He was still feeling the newness of her kiss when Judge Campbell announced they were Dr. and Mrs. Corey Harte.

He was feeling her tongue enter his mouth as Judge Campbell told the officer that he could drive him to the tennis court. And to step on it because Judge Talbot wasn't going to have any advantages.

He sighed with pleasure as Judge Campbell unzipped his robe, revealing white tennis shorts and a tricot jersey shirt.

And he was still kissing his bride when the string quartet began the first triumphant notes of the wedding march and the guests from both sides of the aisle burst into applause.

Epilogue

PRESTON TRUE LAY on the love seat in the kitchen with his feet propped up on cushions and an ice pack held up to his nose.

It was too early to panic, but he was thinking how the really big name stars—Cruise, De Niro, that Baldwin brother—could get away with a broken nose. Chicks still went crazy for them. But a simple caterer in Chicago couldn't. And the best plastic surgeons in the city didn't take insurance—strictly cashier's check or credit card.

His Sulka shirt was swimming in a soup cauldron filled with a salt, vinegar and ice water solution that Aunt Rose swore would get the blood out. But the colors were blurring together in a muddy-colored mess.

He had thought he would be an impressive figure at his friend's party this evening—he had thought wrong. He would look like what he was. A small-time businessman with a broken nose.

"Where's da cake?" a rough voice demanded. "I gotta get a shot of the cake."

"Oh, no, not again," Preston moaned, rising to his feet while keeping the ice pack firmly attached to his nose. He peered out of one side of his face. "What are you doing here?"

"I'm the photographer. I've got exclusives."

"You punched me."

"And I'll do it a second time if you ever open your trap again like that about my friend Corey. Now where's the cake? The guests are done with the chow and they're going to want to dive into this. I want one shot before they do."

"Right there on the table."

"Ah, looks dandy. Six tiers. Can I get a shot with you in there? Take the ice pack off. Oooh, sorry, that schnoz of yours won't shoot well. Where's a knife? We gotta take Bob's name off."

"Don't touch it," Preston snarled, feeling a return of his considerable personal courage and professional integrity. "Stand back, you vulgarian."

"I'm Irish," Rusty pointed out.

Preston put his ice pack down on the counter, took a pastry knife and expertly excised Bob's name.

"It's a confectionery masterpiece." He sighed as Rusty took a picture.

"It is, is it?" Rusty looked speculatively at the cake, spotted a sugared rose to his liking, and used his finger to smear it off with a globule of icing.

Over Preston's horrified gasp, he popped it in his mouth. "Okay, Mr. True, you win. It's good. Real good. By the way, have I ever told you that my wife is the food editor for the *Tribune?*"

The caterer slipped on his silk chef's jacket.

"Why, no, Rusty, my man, you never mentioned it."

"THEY'RE NOT GOING to leave if we don't leave," Robyn said.

Corey wiped a smidgen of icing off her upper lip. "You told me no honeymoon," he said. "So where're we going to go?"

The both glanced out the window. While police had cleared the sidewalk just an hour before, dozens of teens had drifted back—hoping for a glimpse of their idol. Bob and Sarah had only narrowly avoided disaster by sneaking out the back door to Walter Greenough's car with blankets over their heads.

"We could go upstairs," Corey declared. He took her empty plate and punch glass. "You did, after all, marry me."

"I suppose I knew what I was getting into when I walked down the stairs," Robyn conceded.

He picked her up and carried her, to riotous applause, up the stairs to his bedroom.

On the door were six empty aluminum cans hung by crepe paper streamers and a hand-printed sign declaring Just Married, Keep Out!

Corey kicked the door open and brought Robyn to the bed.

"I was looking for those flowers!" Robyn exclaimed.

Corey put her down and picked up the bunch of white tulips held together with a lavender organdy ribbon.

He held them out the door. A cultivated male hand grabbed them.

"Thank you, buddy," Corey said heartily. "For changing the place cards and everything you've done for us since."

"Oh, no, my pleasure," Ashford said. "Gotta go. Lelaine! Lelaine! Catch, darling!"

Corey closed the door and, for good measure, stuck the back of his desk chair under the knob.

"Hold it right there, Corey," Robyn said. He turned around slowly.

She stood by the side of the bed, twisting her sash in her fingers.

"What is it?" he asked, cocking his head.

"I want to hear you say it—now that you have nothing to gain."

He looked at her, puzzled, and then came to a sudden realization. "All right, I'll say it," he said. "But I want you to take your gown off. Now that we're legal. It's a bewitching dress and it's done a lot of magic in its time, but now—" he flicked his thumb towards the floor "—it goes."

She smiled seductively.

"You first."

"Okay. Here goes. I love you," he said.

She reached up over her back and unzipped her-self.

"I love you," he repeated, taking three long strides toward her.

"I love you," he said. Just in case she didn't hear him the first time. Or the second.

She let her gown drop to the floor and he sighed—long and hard.

"Oh, baby," Corey said, slipping his hand down the cool smooth flesh of her back. "Did I ever tell you…I love you?"

They're sexy, they're single, they're daddies...they're

Don't miss a single story as these handsome hunks with kids who warm their heart now find the perfect woman to warm their bed! It's a family in the making—as only Harlequin American Romance can deliver!

Daddy's Little Cowgirl—
available February 1999
by Charlotte Maclay

And be on the lookout for more
SEXY SINGLE DADS!

Available wherever Harlequin books are sold.

He's every woman's fantasy, but only one woman's dream come true.

Harlequin American Romance brings you
THE ULTIMATE...in romance, as our most sumptuous
series continues. Because a guy's wealth, looks and bod
are nothing without that one special woman.

THE ULTIMATE...

...Catch

#760 *RICH, SINGLE & SEXY*
Mary Anne Wilson
January 1999

...*Lover*

#762 *A MAN FOR MEGAN*
Darlene Scalera
February 1999

Don't miss any of The Ultimate...series!

Available at your favorite retail outlet.

COMING NEXT MONTH

#765 THE RIGHT MAN by Anne Stuart
Gowns of White
Five days before Susan Abbott's wedding and she hadn't a thing to
wear. That is until the too-darn-sexy and enigmatic Jake hand delivered an
heirloom wedding gown—and changed her prim and proper, well-planned
life forever.

#766 DADDY'S LITTLE COWGIRL by Charlotte Maclay
Sexy Single Dads
Bad boy turned rancher Reed Drummond had one goal—adopt the tiny
baby girl with whom he'd been entrusted. But to do that, he needed
respectable Ann Forrester to be his wife for a while—or until death do
them part!

#767 BABY FOR HIRE by Liz Ireland
Ross Templeton figured the star baby-model and her nun guardian were
the perfect make-believe daughter and wife he needed. Little did he
know baby Felicity was a terror and that underneath "Sister" Alison's
fake habit beat the heart of a vivacious, sexy woman who could threaten
his bachelor status!

#768 CAN'T RESIST A COWBOY by Jo Leigh
City girl Taylor Reed spared few words for cowboys—arrogant and
pig-headed. She'd come to Zach Baldwin's ranch to prove that cowboys
and marriage didn't mix—and no broad-shouldered, lean-hipped,
sexier-than-he-should-be cowboy was talking her out of it!

Look us up on-line at: http://www.romance.net